An engaging and thoroughly researched story full of telling historical details, *An Abolitionist Family* is especially relevant to today's "cancel," racially divided culture. The struggles of Marty, age 10 at the novel's opening, is an emblematic and realistic portrayal of the pain, suffering and confusion caused by the American Civil War. Marty matures well beyond his years throughout the story's 12-year span as do other characters who, despite their abolitionist leanings, deal with their own innate racism, from interracial romance to the life-threatening consequences of aiding and abetting escaped slaves. Author Barbara Kussow also skillfully interweaves music, literature and appearances by historical figures. Recommended for anyone wanting to understand the underpinnings of racial conflict in America.

- Sandra Gurvis, author of *The Pipe Dreamers, Where have all the Flower Children Gone?* and *Three Ringling Circus: a History of Sarasota, Florida, and the Famous Ringling Brothers.*

AN ABOLITIONIST FAMILY

A Novel of the Civil War Era

BARBARA KUSSOW

ISBN: 978-1-7376076-2-5 (paperback)
ISBN: 978-1-7376076-3-2 (ebook)

For my daughter, Natalie Schneider Nelson, and my mother,

Mary Elizabeth Nichols. They would have been proud.

ACKNOWLEDGMENTS

My gratitude to Sandra Gurvis, John Haueisen, Steffanie Haueisen, Adam G. Kussow, James Kussow, Roger Kussow, Laura Moorman, Richard Schwartz, Joan Trojanowski, Beth Weinhardt, and John Weinhardt for their historical knowledge and technical expertise.

CONTENTS

"An immoral law makes it a man's duty to break it at every
hazard."

Ralph Waldo Emerson, in speech in 1851 opposing the
Fugitive Slave Law

INTRODUCTION

The area around Flint and Park Roads in northern Franklin County has a rich historical background that is not revealed without some effort.

The roads have become heavily traveled, two-lane thoroughfares that connect Ohio State Route 23 with the burgeoning Polaris area and other suburbs. Travelers might glancingly appreciate the quaintness of some older structures, but I dare say, most of them are interested in the area more for its utility than for its history.

Those inclined to take the time for a further look are rewarded with a fascinating glimpse into Ohio's links to the Underground Railroad.

I came to the area's history sideways, so to speak, when I visited Flint Cemetery. I had seen the sign by Flint Road, which is not far from my home. Feeling desolate about not being able to visit a cemetery in a different state where a loved one was laid to rest, I went there to grieve and meditate.

The cemetery is not visible from the road. One must drive a short distance over a narrow bridge that crosses a ravine. Even though the thrum of continual traffic from Flint Road was not far away, the cemetery felt like a secluded haven. No one else was around, and I wandered at my leisure. Exploring the area near the ravine, I was surprised to find many tombstones from the nineteenth century. Some were so weathered the inscriptions were barely legible. Some were toppled or a bit askew; some were small with no inscription.

After that visit, I made it a point to research the cemetery and learn more about the historical significance of the Flint area. The most well-known building on Flint Road is the Ozem Gardner House. I had driven past it numerous times, thinking to myself that it looked like an interesting old house, but until I made a concerted effort to research it, I did not know about its rich history as a stop on the Underground Railroad. Ozem Gardner, was a brickmaker, a farmer, and an abolitionist who is said to have helped more than 200 slaves on their road to freedom. Behind his home was a small structure built into a creek bank where the fugitives took refuge. In 1864, Gardner sold one acre of his land for the Flint Cemetery. He died in 1880 and is buried in the cemetery.

The area was once the site of a small village called Flint, just north of the better-known village of Worthington. Besides the road, the Flint name has been retained by a park, a church, a carry-out store, and, of course, the cemetery. Reportedly, the village was developed mid-century as a railroad stop. (A railroad that crosses Park Road still carries freight trains that cause frequent traffic stops.)

Today, Flint Cemetery is jointly owned and operated by the city of Worthington and Sharon Township. Two "union" cemeteries operate together—the Walnut Ridge Cemetery (Columbus) and the Flint Cemetery. The Gardner House was purchased from a private owner by the Flint cemeteries in 2017. There are plans to restore it to its original appearance. (*This Week – Worthington News*, November 7, 2019).

Ozem Gardner and the Flint environs became the inspiration for *An Abolitionist Family*. In the opening scene, two boys are playing in a ravine. The idea came from the ravine behind the Gardner House and adjacent to the cemetery. As sometimes happens with writers, the scene stayed with me like a recurring song lyric that is hard to ignore.

In a peripheral way, I had been aware of Underground Railroad activity in central Ohio. I knew about the Hanby House in Westerville, Ohio, once the residence of William Hanby, a United Brethren minister, and his family. Reverend Hanby was the co-founder of Otterbein University and an abolitionist. His musician son wrote the song "Darling Nelly Gray," from the point of view of a slave whose beloved is sold to a plantation down the river, a harsher place for slaves.

Popular in the nineteenth century, it became a song for the ages. The Hanby House is now a local historical attraction.

My research told me that abolitionism in the central Ohio area was more prevalent than I realized. Many people helped fugitive slaves. Some are known; some are only speculative. Secrecy was a necessity for the success of the Underground Railroad. I mention Gardner and Hanby specifically because they are well-known and figure in the plot of the book.

As my research gathered momentum and expanded to the state of Ohio, I found myself particularly captivated with the area along the Ohio River. Fugitives often sought a road to freedom by crossing the river from Kentucky, a state that allowed slavery. The town of Ripley was sometimes referred to as a "hot bed of abolitionism." There, abolitionists John Rankin, a Presbyterian minister, and John Parker, a former slave, were prominent. Both are portrayed in interactions with the fictional Spencer family. Today, their houses are historical sites open to the public.

You might say I got hooked on the Underground Railroad. I was intrigued by the people who risked harsh penalties to hide and transport runaway slaves. They did so out of principle because they believed slavery was evil. They thought the Fugitive Slave Act of 1850 was an unjust, immoral law. It required that slaves be returned to their owners, even if they were found in a free state. People who disobeyed the law did so at their peril. They could be harassed, fined large amounts of money, or even imprisoned.

I came to love my characters, the members of the Spencer family. Luke, the father, is upright, principled, and willing to take risks. Virginia, the mother, is calm, steady, and practical. Ed, the oldest brother, is protective and tolerant of his siblings, good at constructing things with his hands, and cool under pressure. Amy is a feisty feminist who loves learning and teaching. Marty, the youngest, is my favorite. Although the novel is written in third person, it focuses on his thoughts and actions. He is ten years old at the start and matures during the twelve-year span of the novel. He is devoted to his family, but he also struggles to be his own person. He can be headstrong. He shows empathy for fugitive slaves and is proud of being reared in an abolitionist family. His relationship with John Parker, the former enslaved man who became a successful business owner in Ripley, Ohio, is a highlight of the book.

The music and literature of the age are other avenues I used to show the temper of the time. Harriet Beecher Stowe's novel *Uncle Tom's Cabin*, the poetry of John Whittier, the anti-slavery letters of John Rankin, and the autobiography of Stephen Douglass enhance the abolitionist theme.

As I wrote this novel, I became sensitized to current news and commentary that show race controversies are still prevalent and volatile in America. Alarmingly, some media pundits and highly partisan citizens have expounded on the possibility of another civil war. The cacophony of thorny racial issues and conflicting political views made my nineteenth century novel seem relevant to the twenty-first century. I will mention, without editorializing, some of the controversies and catchphrases that captured headlines: the "Black Lives Matter" movement (and especially the murder of George Floyd aired on television for millions of viewers to see), "Defund the Police"; Critical Race Theory; the 1619 Project; the removal of Confederate statues; the voting rights issue; the White Supremacy movement; and, in general, the clashes and incidents taking place in marches and protests.

A contemporary piece of writing deeply moved me was an essay by the poet Caroline Randall Williams, that appeared in the *New York Times* on June 26, 2020. It is titled "You Want a Confederate Monument? My Body is a Confederate Monument." Williams writes in searing, concrete language about her mixed-race heritage. Mixed-race is a subordinate theme of this novel. John Parker and Frederick Douglass are mulattos; so is Aron, one of the main fictional characters.

Williams describes her mixed-race heritage in this way: "I have rape-colored skin. My light-brown-blackness is a living testament to the rules, the practices, the causes of the Old South."

A final thought: The irony is that I, a person who was too faint-hearted to watch Ken Burns's television series on the Civil War, have written a novel about the era—albeit through the narrower lens of the Underground Railroad.

PART I:
ANTEBELLUM
(1854-1860)

1854

Encounter in the Ravine, Worthington, Ohio

Two boys played in a ravine on a muggy August day.

In rainy seasons, the water in the ravine rose to the level of a small creek, but on that day, it was low enough for the boys to wade in, hop from one rock to another, and move rocks about.

Marty, age 10, lived in a home on the hill above the ravine. He wore a battered hat that was too large for his small face, but it protected his light-skinned complexion from the sun. The other boy named Aron was about the same age. He had olive skin and curly hair. His hair, not his facial features, identified him as possibly a mulatto.

Suddenly, Marty became still and cocked his head, "Yuh hear that noise? It sounds like horses' hooves clip-clopping on rocks. They're comin' toward us."

He wondered why riders were in the ravine and not on the road. Why were they picking their way around rocks in the ravine when they could be riding out in the open where the ground was smoother?

Bone, Marty's dog, started growling.

"Sh-h, Bone, you gotta behave!" He tucked his tail and looked at Marty sheepishly.

Marty felt uneasy and started to tell Aron they should run, but then he stopped. He judged from the sound that the riders were near enough that they might catch sight of them running.

Aron wasn't supposed to be outside, so if they acted like they had something to hide, that wouldn't be good. It may also have been curiosity or even a taste for adventure that made him stay put. At any rate, he knew it wouldn't be good for them to scrutinize Aron. He plucked the hat off his head and put it on Aron.

"Why you do that?" He gaped at Marty, open-mouthed.

"Sh-h. Jus' be quiet and let me do the talkin'!" He used the tone his daddy used when he meant business.

The men stopped near them. One was big, not fat, just big—tall and wide. His horse looked tired from carrying all that weight, his own plus a large, worn saddle and saddlebags with a rifle in a scabbard. He had a salt-and-pepper beard and sharp, black eyes that stared at the boys from under a wide-brimmed hat. The other man was thin, like he didn't get enough to eat. His eyes were pale gray and watery. Marty thought he looked like a man who tried to sell his family a cure-all potion in town one day. He also wore a hat and carried a pistol in a holster around his waist. His eyes slid right over Marty like a waterfall and landed on Aron and stayed there. They both looked like men who didn't have homes, or if they did have homes, they didn't spend much time in them.

"What you boys doin' here?" the big man asked. His eyes seemed to pierce right through Marty.

"We're buildin' a dam," said Marty.

"Don't look like a puny stream like this needs a dam."

"We're just pretendin'."

He stared at Aron. "Hey boy, don't you talk?"

Aron shook his head.

"He's shy," Marty said. "He's my cousin, just staying with us for a while because my aunt, his mama, is awful sick." The lie was as easy as melting butter.

"His skin is diff'rent from yours—kind of dark. He ain't one of them half breeds, is he?"

"No sir, he ain't that. That's for sure!" Marty wasn't even sure exactly what a half breed was.

"Is that your house up there?" He pointed to the house on the hill.

"Yes sir, it sure is." All the "yes sirs" were his strategy of politeness, which his mama always told him will take him a long way in life.

And just then Marty's mama started callin' him.

"Mar-tin! Mar-tin! Answer me. Do you hear me?"

"Comin' Mama," he yelled as loud as he could.

The big man's horse snorted and pawed the ground, like the shouting got him excited. The man jerked the reins to make him behave.

Aron and Marty scrambled up the slope with Bone bounding ahead of them. Marty's heart was in his throat. He was grateful for his mama's call.

He shoved Aron in the back door. "Go to the cellar and stay there, you hear!" He was afraid that Amy, his older sister, would be in the kitchen. She would know he'd broken the rule about not taking Aron outside and might tell on him. He got a break. She must be outside with their mama.

He went around the house to the south side to find them in the garden.

"Where have you been, young man? You know your daddy asked you to hoe the beans today. And go check on Aron. I haven't seen him since breakfast."

"Okay but let me get my hat first. Sun's awful bright today."

In the house, he went straight to the window that gave him the best view of the ravine. The men were riding up the hill on the north side of the house. Once, they stopped and looked at the house. He ducked so they wouldn't see him. He wondered if they were thinking about coming to the house. His daddy wasn't home to handle things. *Please God make them go on,* he prayed silently. And his prayer was answered. After a short time, they started toward the road. He found his hat on a kitchen chair, but Aron was nowhere to be seen. He figured he'd followed his orders and was hiding out in the basement. At least it was cool down there. He'd be out workin' in the hot sun.

Later, he went to the basement and gave Aron a talking-to.

"Those men we met today—they might be slave hunters."

"You mean looking for my mama."

"Yes—and looking for you."

His eyes widened. "My mama, she jus say she goin' somewhere and want me with her. She said the man who live in the big house might be lookin' for her and we have to hide."

"If they're lookin' for her, they're probably lookin' for you, too. Understand? They'll tie you up and take you back to the plantation where you lived."

"I jus' wanna be with my mama. She tell me what to do."

Your mama had to leave because she was in danger. Men like we saw today might be lookin' for her. You were sick, and we kept you here until you got well and we can take you to a place where you might be with your mama again. You understand?"

A tear rolled down his cheek. "I, I'm scared."

"I am, too. My family … we're tryin' to take care of you, make you free."

The word "free" sounded funny on his tongue, but it also made him feel he was doing something important. He guessed that's the way his mama and daddy felt when they got in the business of helping Mr. Gardner, who they call an abolitionist. They said that he was a person who believed that slavery should be abolished and that runaway slaves should be helped to escape owners who made them work for no money and were sometimes mean to them.

"Anyway, we have to be very careful. We can't go outside no more. You have to stay hidden. Understand?"

He nodded.

∞ ∞ ∞

Marty had a hard time sleeping that night.

In the middle of the night, he woke with a start. He was sure the two men were in their yard. They were trying to get in through a window on the side of the house opposite his room.

He felt the full impact of the encounter in the ravine—what might have happened or what he may have set in motion. He wanted to scream—to run into his parents' room and shake them awake.

But he shook off the fog and the terror and knew he'd had a nightmare. He lit the candle on his bedside table. He felt he had to check on Aron in the basement.

Bone was lying at the foot of his bed as usual. He raised his head and looked at him as if to ask, "Why are you up at this time of night?"

The light from the candle woke Aron immediately. He tried to jump up from his pallet on the floor, struggling with the tangle of blankets.

His eyes were shiny with fear.

When he realized it was Marty, his body slackened a bit, but he asked, "Is they come?"

"No, Aron, it's just me." Then he added, "I'm just looking for something I need. You can go back to sleep." It was another easy lie.

He lay down again on the hay Amy and Marty had brought into the basement because, for some reason, it made Aron feel safe. Shortly after Aron came to them, he disappeared. The family was afraid he'd gone off by himself trying to find his mama or was hiding out in the woods. They found him lying in hay in the barn. They told him he had to sleep in the basement, but he stubbornly refused. Then, Amy had an idea. She said maybe he'd slept on hay in his cabin on the plantation where he came from. Their mama had grumbled about the mess but let them bring it in the house anyway. After that, Aron slept in the basement.

Upstairs, Marty looked at the grandfather clock in the hallway. It was 2 a.m.

Why did I do this? he asked himself. Wake him up? Scare him? Now, he was afraid Aron might do something stupid like run away from their house. He muttered his question to himself: "Is they come?" He'd seen the fear in his eyes. Maybe he thought they couldn't keep him safe any longer.

Marty was afraid he'd put his family in danger. He loved his family dearly and was proud of them. There were five, including himself. Edward, his older brother, usually called Ed, just turned seventeen. Amy, his sister, was fifteen. Their parents were Luke and Virginia Spencer. Their farm was on the outskirts of Worthington, Ohio, a town near Columbus, the State capital. The town was named after Thomas Worthington who was one of Ohio's first Senators when Ohio became a state in 1803. Then, some years later, he became Governor. Mr. Spencer said the people who settled in Worthington came from New England and most were against slavery from the start.

Marty was spooked, and he knew he'd have to do what he dreaded. He'd have to fess up to his mama and daddy, in the morning. He woke up early, nervous but determined to face the music.

In the past, his daddy had threatened to get his strap out to discipline him, but he couldn't ever remember him actually using it. He wondered about Ed. Was Ed ever whupped before he came along. He doubted it. Their daddy's stares were enough to scare them. When he got the stare, Marty felt his daddy could see right into his black soul.

His father also had other ways of discipline. The maddest Marty had ever seen him at Ed—calling him by his full name, Edward James Spencer—was when Marty fell off the roan horse and broke his leg. He'd been riding behind Ed, with arms around his waist. He thought he was holding on tight, but the roan reared up when a rabbit crossed its path, and down he went. Mr. Spencer had warned Ed that the roan was temperamental, but Ed had been trying to gentle him. He called him Rollie.

Anyway, Marty broke his right leg, and it never healed properly. He still walked with a slight limp, and it ached when it rained. His father roared like thunder at Ed, and Ed gave him some sass back, saying that any horse could be spooked by a rabbit. But Marty didn't blame Ed. Marty never told his father that he had begged Ed to let him ride. He tried to tell him once, but he wouldn't listen.

Two weeks after the accident, Mr. Spencer sold the roan. The day he was sold, Ed disappeared into the woods and didn't come back for supper. Mrs. Spencer left him a plate of fried chicken, mashed potatoes, and green beans. It was after dark when Ed finally returned. He didn't touch the food and went straight to bed. His eyes were red and bleary, and Marty knew he'd been crying.

The next morning, their mother scolded him for being late and wasting good food. She said maybe he should have his cold supper for breakfast. Their father didn't say anything.

A few weeks later, Mr. Spencer brought Bone home. They needed a watch dog, he said, but Marty thought Bone was sort of a replacement for Rollie. Bone was a handsome collie. His body was mostly black with white legs and a white ruff hanging from his neck and shoulders. He had black ears with some tan fur around his eyes and jaws that made his black eyes stand out.

Ed ignored Bone for a couple of months. Bone didn't understand. He had a sheepish, pleading look around Ed, like what have I done wrong that this person doesn't like me.

Finally, Ed relented. He started teaching Bone tricks, like how to stand up and beg for treats. Though Bone slept with Marty at night, he started following Ed during the day when he was around.

Marty's Confession

Marty thought about asking for a family meeting before his father went out to plow the fields. But that made him feel all twitchy. Only his parents had done that and even they hadn't done it very often.

He ate part of his scrambled eggs and then just blurted it out. Well, blurted, sort of … He had a slight stutter that got worse when he was put on the spot.

"I- I need to tell you something about Aron, Aron and me."

Amy looked at him and arched her eyebrows. He scowled at her. *Miss know-it-all!* He plunged ahead.

"Ar-Aron, he was unhappy because he can't go outside. He- he begged me to take him down to the creek, just for a few minutes." He went silent.

His father said, "But you told him that wasn't allowed."

It wasn't a question. Marty took a deep breath.

"Well, I- I know it was wrong, but I- I felt sorry for him, and I- I guess I did it."

"You guess?"

"O-okay, I- I did it, and I- I'm sorry."

"There's more to this story, ain't there?"

"Well …"

"Go ahead."

"Well … some men came riding up the creek bed. I- I thought, thought they could be men like what you've told us about—slave hunters. I- I thought we should run, but then I thought they might see us run and that, that would make it worse. I- I was wearing your old straw hat, with the hole in the brim, And I took it off and put it on Aron--you know because he's so, so light-skinned. I- I thought all I need to do is cover his, cover his curly hair. But, but they kept looking at him …"

His father demanded that he tell exactly what happened. Then, he got quiet and studied him.

"Why did you decide to fess up about this?"

"Because, because … I'm afraid, I'm afraid they m-might come back."

"You're right about that. I think we need to act immediately. I'll need to talk to Gardner to see what we can work out. Meanwhile, Martin, get yourself to the field and do my plowing."

Aron's Departure

Mr. Spencer took off in the buggy.

When Marty came in for lunch, his father was back and all keyed up.

"Gardner says we should get Aron out as soon as possible. We're going to do it after lunch. It's daytime, and we'd ordinarily wait until dark to try something, but we need to make haste. And slave hunters probably won't be expectin' us to do it in broad daylight. Here's the plan. I borrowed a buggy with a false bottom. We've got to get Aron into the bottom. Everybody has to help."

"What do you want us to do, Luke?" Mrs. Spencer asked.

"I'm gonna drive the buggy inside the barn and load some hay in it. I want all of you to help. Ed, I want you to be a scout. Go look around in the ravine and woods to see if you see anybody lurking on our property. Virginia, I want you and Amy to find a dress that we can get Aron into. Aron is about Amy's size and height. Find him a dress and a bonnet that will cover his head. Maybe use some powder or flour on his face. Martin, I want you to explain to Aron what's going on and help him get dressed. Walk with him to the barn, and we'll get him in the bottom of the buggy."

Marty couldn't believe it. "You're gonna dress him up like a girl?"

"That's what I just said."

Ed asked, "Why do I need to scout if he's gonna be disguised?"

"Just an extra precaution. I'd just like to know if anybody's watchin', or maybe wants to follow us," his father said.

When Marty told Aron what he'd have to do, he wrinkled his nose. "You wanna put me in a dress!" Marty almost smiled but knew he shouldn't because this was serious. He thought to himself, even a slave boy has his pride.

"That's what Daddy said to do. If, if someone's watchin' our house, you should be disguised when we walk to the barn. They'll think you're my sister. He says it's very important to take you away from here because he thinks the men were slave catchers, and they'll probably come back. We, we can't take any chances."

"What's gonna happen to me? Will I be able to see Mama?"

"Well, maybe, maybe not for a while, but there will be people who will help you travel north to Canada where she is now. People will help you find her."

He didn't know if this was true, but he felt he had to say it to get him to do what needed to be done. Mrs. Spencer brought a dress and bonnet down the stairs, and Marty helped Aron get dressed. He wanted to wear the dress over his clothes, but that didn't work. Marty looked around the basement and found a basket to put his clothes in. All Aron had was a shirt and pants, and Marty wondered if he might get cold on the trip wherever he was going because the shirt was kind of thin.

"Just wait here for me. I'll be right back."

He ran upstairs and found one of Ed's old wool shirts with long sleeves and stuck it in the basket.

"This is a warm shirt in case you get cold. You, you can change back into your clothes when they tell you it's safe." He didn't know who *they* might be.

They went upstairs, where Amy powdered Aron's face, although there wasn't much of his face showing. Mrs. Spencer said, "Now, Aron, I want you to stand very straight like Amy."

They started walking to the barn. Marty avoided looking at Aron and tried to act as he might act if he were walking with Amy. Aron squeezed himself into the small space in the bottom of the buggy. He looked frightened.

"Don't worry. You won't be in here long." Again, he wasn't sure he was telling him the truth. His soul was getting blacker and blacker what with his, not lies exactly, but makin' stuff up because of what his father said was an emergency.

Ed picked up the basket of clothes and tried to put it in the space, but it wouldn't go. So, he just took the clothes out of the basket and shoved them in with Aron. "Here, put these under your head to be more comfortable."

He looked at Marty. "Little brother, that's one of my favorite shirts."

"Yeah, it's warm now, but he might get cold in Canada …"

He gave him a look that said he was a big bother, but Marty knew he didn't mind too much.

When he saw the buggy roll through the gate loaded with hay and Aron, Marty muttered a prayer to himself. *Please God, please keep Daddy and Aron safe, and also please let what I said about Aron's mama come true.*

Aron and Dora

Aron and his mama came to the Spencer house about four or five months earlier in the wintertime. As far as the Spencer children knew, it was the first time the family had helped runaway slaves—although they suspected their father might have helped Mr. Gardner, who it was whispered had helped many runaways.

Aron's mama was a tall woman, who held herself in a proud, dignified way. Mrs. Spencer said she looked regal, like an African queen. She told them her name was Dora, but otherwise, she didn't talk much. She stayed in the basement with Aron and didn't like to come upstairs even for a short time. Amy said she was mysterious, and that made her determined to make friends with her. She asked her lots of questions. Dora gradually began to talk to Amy more than anybody.

His mama's skin was a shade darker than Aron's but still not as dark as some Negroes.

Marty asked his mother why Aron's skin was so light. She pretended like she didn't hear him. When he asked again, she told him she didn't know and that it was none of his business anyway.

Later, he asked Amy, who seemed to know everything. She got that look in her eye that said she knew a secret that shouldn't be talked about.

"Come on, I can tell you know somethin'."

"I'm not supposed to know, but I learned from my friend at school—not about Aron and his mama specifically—but about how white slave owners who, who have children with their slaves…"

"What?" That just didn't sound right to Marty.

"Yes, my friend Ann learned that from her mama who was not afraid to talk about it. I asked Ed if he'd heard anything about this happening. Ed asked Daddy, who told him the truth. He said that that sometimes owners make babies with their slave women, and when their children are born, they don't even claim them. The children are called mulattos and grow up as slaves."

This was something Marty didn't want to know, didn't think was possible. He could feel himself blushing.

"I-I don't believe that!" He turned and walked away. But at night when he lay in bed and thought about it, he knew it must be true.

He couldn't imagine Amy having such a conversation with Ed or Ed having such a conversation with their father. It made him feel like he was a baby who got left out of things, and he didn't want everybody to think of him as a little kid anymore.

Amy learned that Dora had been a "house Negro." That meant she worked inside the house doing stuff like cooking and cleaning and washing clothes. She didn't work out in the cotton fields, and Amy believed she held herself above the field Negroes.

When Amy discovered that Aron had never gone to school, she was angry because she said every child should be allowed to go to school. Amy wanted to be a teacher. She attended the Worthington Female Seminary, where she learned basic things like reading, writing, and arithmetic, but also fancy stuff like art and music and poetry and French.

Amy vowed to teach Aron to read and write. She set up school in the basement. Ed, who was good at making things. brought in two sawhorses and laid a wide plank on them. That was the desk. Then, they needed stools, so she had him make two wooden stools.

Amy began to realize that Dora hadn't had much schooling either. She only could spell a few words that she'd learned working in the plantation mansion. She'd taught Aron how to spell his name, but they didn't have any books or slate boards or chalk or anything. She wrote it out in the dirt with a stick. Dora began to pay attention to Amy's lessons, and she seemed happier. Both were learning.

Sometimes, Amy gave progress reports at dinner. For instance, she said Aron had trouble understanding how a small map drawing could represent a big country. She was trying to show him where Canada was because he and his mama might go there. She asked him if he'd ever been on a boat in the river. He said yes. She showed him the line on the map that was the Ohio River and told him Canada was like that—little on the map, but really a big country. Dora seemed excited and asked questions about Canada that Amy couldn't answer.

Marty and Amy decided it wasn't much fun for Aron and Dora to be cooped up in the basement all the time, and they came up with some things to entertain them. Ed had Bone do tricks, and Aron laughed out loud. It was the first time anyone heard him laugh. Amy and Marty showed him how to play checkers and Dora watched while he and Marty played and helped him make some moves to beat Marty, but first thing he knew, Aron really was good enough to beat him. Amy had a good voice and sang in the church choir. She thought about singing, but then, couldn't find something suitable. Hymns wouldn't do because she wanted to sing something light and happy. Finally, she settled on reading a poem called "The Day is Done," by Henry Wadsworth Longfellow:

> *The day is done, and the darkness*
> *Falls from the wings of night ,*
> *As a feather is wafted downward*
> *From an eagle in his flight.*
>
> *I see the lights of the village*
> *Gleam through the rain and the mist,*
> *And a feeling of sadness comes o'er me*
> *That my soul cannot resist:*

Marty didn't understand its meaning, but it was nice to listen to. Amy said she chose it because she could picture a runaway tramping through the forest in the rain and then seeing the lights of a village through the mist.

Marty really liked the words of the last verse

> *... cares, that infest the day,*
> *Shall fold their tents, like the Arabs,*
> *And as silently steal away.*

Amy told him it was like slaves silently stealing away in the night.

Then, one day, Aron and Dora surprised them. They sang a hymn together. Their voices were soft and sad:

> *I looked over Jordan and what did I see*
> *Coming for to carry me home*
> *A band of angels coming after me*
> *Coming for to carry me home*
>
> *If you get there before I do*
> *Coming for to carry me home*
> *Tell all my friends I'm coming, too*
> *Coming for to carry me home*
>
> *Swing low, sweet chariot*
> *Coming for to carry me home*
> *Swing low, sweet chariot*
> *Coming for to carry me home.*

Later, their father told them he thought the hymn might have another meaning other than religion and heaven. He said he'd heard it might be about slaves yearning for freedom and Jordan might mean the Ohio River.

Amy immediately said that was what is called a metaphor—a word no one knew but her. She said it's when one thing means something else.

About a month after Amy started having school, Aron came down with a fever and a bad cold. It might be pneumonia, Mrs. Spencer said. His mama held him curled up against her on the pallet. She stroked his head, and sometimes he moaned, and she moaned. She was afraid he was going to die, Amy said. Mrs. Spencer brought cool washcloths to put on his forehead, an ointment for Dora to rub on his chest, and chicken broth for him to sip.

Aron was a little better but still not well one night Mr. Gardner turned up at their house. He was alarmed because he'd gotten word that Dora's owner had offered a big reward for her, and several slave hunters were on the prowl. He believed he had a chance to get her out safely, but they would have to make haste.

It was decided that Dora should go but Aron would stay because he wasn't well enough to travel. Dora cried and said no, she didn't want to leave without Aron. Mr. Gardner took her aside and talked to her quietly for several minutes and finally she gave in. He promised that they'd try to get Aron out soon and that people would look after him and he would be with her in Canada.

Family Meeting

When Mr. Spencer returned from spiriting Aron away, he said they would have a family meeting after dinner.

Marty thought, uh oh, here it comes. He would be dressed down in front of the family because he had disobeyed his parents and taken Aron outside. He remembered what he'd been taught in Sunday school: "Honor thy father and thy mother." He didn't mean to, but maybe he had broken a commandment.

Instead, his father started out by saying that the family was new to slave-hiding, and he wanted them to know how proud he was of all of them for the way they treated Aron and his mother, Dora. He praised his wife for helping nurse Aron back to health. He praised Amy for her basement school and Ed for helping her set it up. He said Marty was a good friend to Aron, and even though he had disobeyed the rule by taking him outside, he'd done some quick thinking when he met the slave hunters. He said that the fact that the slave hunters were on their land probably meant that they had some inkling that slaves were being held, if not in their house, then somewhere nearby. The reason he'd helped by hiding them in their house in the first place was because Mr. Gardner had gotten word that there were slave hunters in the area, and he felt his own home and grounds might be under suspicion.

Then, Mr. Spencer got solemn and serious.

"Slave-hiding can be a dangerous business. Slave hunters sometimes get violent. There is some loose talk about war between slavers and non-slavers and about southern states seceding—leaving the Union and setting up their own government.

"I could get in big trouble. There's a law. It was pushed through Congress by the slavers. It's called the Fugitive Slave Act. It says that all escaped slaves must be returned to their masters and that citizens in Free states must cooperate. I could be subject to a $1,000 fine and six months in jail if I were found guilty of helping a slave. It's sometimes called the Bloodhound Law because slave hunters use dogs to hunt slaves."

Marty shivered. He imagined Aron and Dora being chased by dogs that jumped on them, biting them and tearing at their clothes. He thought about Bone and what a good dog he was, gentle with the family but fierce if he thought someone might do them harm—like those slave hunters.

"Why …? Ed's voice trailed off.

"Why did I agree to hide people like Aron and Dora, if there are such harsh punishments? Well, I know it's takin' a chance, but many people ignore the law. It's a bad law and it's not often enforced. We believe that we answer to a higher law. I just believe helping people escape slavery is the right thing to do. Now, mind you, we are still a law-abidin' family otherwise."

"Will we be hiding more people?" Ed asked.

"Well, I don't know that now. I know I've said this before, but I want to tell you again. All of you must keep quiet about our activities and beliefs against slavery. I don't want to put you in danger--but we can talk about it as a family."

Amy spoke up. "Daddy, I read a book that shows how awful slavery is. It's fiction, a made-up story, but the characters and the things that happen to them are like what happens in real life."

Mr. Spencer swiveled his head at her in surprise. "And what book would that be, Miss Amy?"

"*Uncle Tom's Cabin.* It's written by a woman, Harriet Beecher Stowe." Marty could tell by her voice that she was proud a woman wrote it.

"I've heard of that book. Where did you get it?" their mother asked.

"I borrowed it from my friend, Ann. Her mother bought it somewhere."

"Maybe we can get our own copy. It would be nice if you could read it aloud to the family," her mother added.

Unwanted Visitors

"Is they come?"

They did come. The next day the men showed up early on their doorstep.

Mr. Spencer grabbed his rifle and stepped outside to talk to them but left the door ajar. Ed and Marty listened to them. Mr. Spencer didn't aim the rifle at them. He just pointed it at the ground and leaned on it. He asked them their names and what their business was. They told him that they were in the business of hunting fugitive slaves. They had the right by law to look for them and return them to their owners. Bone started growling.

The big man, who had introduced himself as Manson, said their family was suspected of harboring a fugitive and they wanted to search their house. Mr. Spencer argued with them, saying they had no right to violate the family's privacy. There was a back-and-forth like this for a while. Marty was afraid they might force their way into the house.

Manson said if they couldn't come in, they would report their suspicions to the authorities and ask that the house be put under surveillance. He warned Mr. Spencer that he could be fined as much as a thousand dollars and could serve time in prison for helping a fugitive slave.

Ed and Marty looked at each other. They knew about the Fugitive Slave Act because their father had explained it to them the night before. Then, the man tried a different tack. His voice became less threatening. He said if they had any slaves to turn over to them, he would see that there were no penalties. Everything would be done on the quiet.

Mr. Spencer told them again that there were no fugitives in their house. They finally turned and stomped away, saying they would come back with a U.S. marshal who would let them do the search.

Afterwards, Ed asked their father why he just didn't let them come in because they no longer had any fugitives in the house. He said, "It's the principle, Ed. It's the principle of the thing."

The U.S. Marshal showed up a week later. Mr. Spencer treated him differently than he did the slave hunters. He invited him in, and Mrs. Spencer asked him if he'd like some tea and cookies. He accepted, and he and Mr. Spencer talked about crops and weather.

He showed him around the house, including the basement and the attic. They had made sure that both were what Mr. Spencer said was beyond suspicion. They'd even moved some dusty, broken furniture to the attic. They'd been storing a broken chair and dresser in the barn. Ed had thought maybe he might restore them someday.

The Marshal asked why he had refused to let the slave hunters search the house. Mr. Spencer told him what he told his family. It was a matter of privacy and principle. Just before he left, the Marshal asked Mr. Spencer if he was aware of the provisions of the Fugitive Slave Act. He warned him that it wasn't worth the risk to hide slaves.

Abolitionist Tales

After that, Mr. Spencer started talking to his children more about slave hunting and abolition. It was like a dam had broken. They found out that he'd attended some meetings of a group called the Anti-Slavery Society, and he knew quite a bit about people who helped fugitive slaves—a lot more than his children suspected. Mrs. Spencer never seemed surprised at anything he said, so the children thought the two of them had probably had many private conversations. Every night at supper, they had a conversation that went on long after they'd finished eating. Mrs. Spencer would get impatient and start clearing the dishes away and shoo them out of the kitchen.

He said they must solemnly vow not to talk to anyone about people helping runaways. "There's a lot of people who hold different views. Some think that the Fugitive Slave law should be obeyed. Some don't like colored people, and some would help slave hunters to get part of a reward. When I tell you these things, I'm treating you as grown-ups and trusting you. People could get harmed, and slaves would no longer have safe places, if abolitionists are exposed."

Of course, they knew about Mr. Ozem Gardner. He lived near them, and they knew their father helped him by hiding Aron and Dora. Mr. Gardner was a brick mason who worked on many buildings in Worthington and Columbus. "He believes he's helped over 100 runaways over the years," their father told them. He said Mr. Gardner also had a big garden and sold his produce. Sometimes, he used his wagon with the false bottom and covered the fugitives with fruits and vegetables. Other people who sometimes helped him transport runaways were a man named Ansel Matoon and a free slave known as Ole Black Joe. "And 'course, there's us."

Their father told them about a minister named John Rankin who had given sermons on the evils of slavery all over Ohio. He had heard him speak one time.

"Reverend Rankin and his family live in Ripley, Ohio, a town on the Ohio River, not far from where your Uncle Seth lives." Seth Porter was their mother's brother.

"On the other side of the river is the state of Kentucky which is a slave-holding state where runaways often ford the river to escape. It is known that the Rankins have helped many fugitive slaves. They light a lamp in a front window at night that acts as a beacon. Their home is a prime target for slave hunters. One night, they attacked Reverend Rankin's home. Fortunately, he had grown sons who were able to thwart the attack, and thank God, no one was hurt. But shots were fired, and the slave hunters started a fire near his barn."

He said Reverend Rankin wrote a series of letters to his brother about the evils of slavery when he found out that he bought some slaves. The letters had been published for a wider audience. Their father didn't have copies of them but said he would get them and read some of them to the family.

A few days later, he brought the letters of Reverend Rankin and read passages from them:

> *The Africans are deeply degraded. The hand of oppression has pressed them down from the rank of men to that of beasts; they are bought and sold and driven from place to place like mere animal herds; this fetters the mind, and prevents that expansion of soul which dignifies man and ornaments civilized life.*
>
> *They seldom have any opportunities of improvement, any encouragement for the efforts of genius, or any inducements to enter the field of science. Hence, in many instances, the strongest powers of mind remain unfolded; over them oppression draws her sable mantle, on them she lays her cruel hand, and forbids them ever to rise.*

Marty went to bed with those words ringing in his head. He thought they were the most powerful words he'd ever heard. He wanted his father to read more of the letters.

∞ ∞ ∞

One night, their father said, "Let me tell you about the President of the Underground Railroad."

"Huh?"

Mr. Spencer smiled. He liked to surprise them.

"You might say our house has become a station on the Underground Railroad. It's a term I've heard used to describe the network of people and places that help hide runaways. 'Course, it's not a real railroad. Some people say people started using the description when a man who was tracking his slave crossed the river and disappeared suddenly. He said, 'It's like he found an underground road!'"

"But who is President of the Underground Railroad?" Marty was impatient to know who had such a noble title.

"A man named Levi Coffin is sometimes called that by slavers. He is of the Quaker religion. I would say that most Quakers believe slavery is a moral issue and should be abolished, even though there are some Quakers who own slaves. Mr. Coffin lived in Indiana, where he helped hundreds, if not thousands, of runaways. Then, he moved to Cincinnati, where he runs a store that sells only goods that are not made from slave labor, and he's still involved in the Underground Railroad."

Their mother got up and began to remove the dishes from the table, a big hint for them to leave the kitchen.

"Remember, we talked about how many slaves cross the Ohio River. Well, Cincinnati is on the Ohio River, too."

Are there any Quaker abolitionists around here?" Ed asked

"Yes, indeed." He paused. "But I must caution you again not to talk about Quakers or others about abolitionism. The only way the movement can be effective is if things are done secretly. We can't have loose tongues, understand?"

They all nodded solemnly.

He told them that there were several Quaker abolitionists in Delaware County, north of Worthington, and a settlement of Quakers in Alum Creek, some twenty-five miles from their house, who were probably involved in the Underground Railroad.

One night Ed asked him, "Are we going to hide more runaways?"

Mr. Spencer said he wasn't sure, but later they got their answer when he proposed a cold weather project. He wanted Ed to use his carpentry skills to finish the attic, including making a false closet. The attic had joists or beams that ran across it with what their father called a catwalk, a walkway about two feet wide that they could walk across to get to the end where there was a storage place. In the winter, they spread some old woolen blankets in the area to help keep out the cold. Their father wanted to add more boards to the catwalk to make a floor and build a false closet in the storage place.

So, Ed built the hidden closet behind the real closet. It was a beautiful thing. A person couldn't tell from looking at it how to open it, and he made it hard to open. It looked like a wall but not a new wall. He used older boards so it wouldn't look like something he'd just built. So, now they had a false closet and a false wagon bed. Well, the wagon wasn't really theirs. It belonged to Mr. Gardner.

1855

School Troubles

In March, Marty spent his days in school thinking about things other than his lessons. Amy loved school and wanted to go to college. He wondered how Ed felt about school. Ed never talked about school. He'd quit going at age 14 and never talked about it. Marty thought maybe he just went along with it and knew he would be doing something in the future to use his skills for making and fixing things. Amy was good at school and teaching; Ed was good with his hands. Marty wasn't particularly good at anything that he could think of.

When he was supposed to be concentrating on math, he stared out the window and saw that it was snowing. He wished he were home. He'd be on the long sled with Bone sitting in front of him. Ed had taught Bone to ride on the sled, and he pulled them or sometimes pushed them down a small hill. Bone's fur and ears flew back in the wind. It reminded Marty of a sail on a boat he saw when the family visited Lake Erie last summer. Sometimes Bone jumped off before they reached the bottom of the hill, but then he ran to the top of the hill and wanted to do it again.

Marty dozed off and woke when Mr. Pitts gave him a sharp rap on the shoulder with his ruler. "I want to see the answers to those math problems in 15 minutes, Mr. Spencer."

Still groggy, he muttered, "My daddy doesn't hit me with a ruler." He hated it when Mr. Pitts called him Mr. Spencer. Grownups were addressed as Mr. or Mrs.

"What did you say, Young Martin?"

"Noth, Nothing'."

"Yes, it was something. I want to know what you said!"

"Well, I, I said my daddy doesn't hit me with a ruler."

"Well, maybe he should! You were disrespectful. You will plan to stay an hour after school for the rest of the week and keep me company while I work on preparing lessons."

When he got home that afternoon, it was beginning to get dark. His mother was worried about him. He didn't want to tell her what happened, but finally she got it out of him.

The next day, Mr. Spencer turned up at school right after the other kids were dismissed. Mr. Pitts rose from his desk, surprised. Mr. Spencer reached out his hand to shake Mr. Pitts' hand. He asked in a calm voice why Marty was staying late after school, and Mr. Pitts told him what he'd said after he rapped his shoulder.

"Well, he was telling the truth. I don't rap him on the shoulder."

"You don't spank him, or use a strap on him?" Mr. Pitts asked.

"No. Now there may have been times when I felt like it. But Martin's a good kid. He tries to do what is right. Maybe he shouldn't fall asleep in class, but I can see that would happen if he's tired."

"He disrespected me by sassing me, and he should learn that he can't disrespect a teacher or any elder. You don't want him to grow up to be a rebel, do you?" He made the word "rebel" sound like Marty might turn out to be a criminal.

Mr. Spencer ignored the question.

"Martin is needed at home after school to help with chores. It isn't good for him to get home so late."

That wasn't exactly true. Marty tagged along after Ed and him while they did most of the chores, but he did do things like carry logs into the house for the stove and fireplace.

Mr. Pitts wasn't happy about it, but he agreed to keep Marty only one more day after school instead of the whole week. It was Tuesday, so, at least, his father got him out of Thursday and Friday's punishment. After that, Mr. Pitts never rapped him with his ruler again, although he did rap his desk a couple of times. Marty suspected that he always called on him to answer hard questions and took satisfaction when he didn't have the right answers. His father had made it clear to him that he was to obey Mr. Pitts and not do any more "rebel behavior." So, he just took satisfaction in thinking to himself that Mr. Pitts was the kind of man who, if he knew they hid runaway slaves, he'd probably find a way to inform slave hunters or a U.S. Marshal.

Joseph

Joseph came to them at the end of March. They put him in the attic and showed him the false closet and how to open it. He could go in it if needed. Though the attic was chilly, there was a window at the south end so he could get some sun, and he had blankets to keep him warm. Mr. Spencer gave him a stern lecture about not going near the window lest slave hunters were watching the house.

He was a skinny guy maybe 30 years old, with big eyes that seemed ready to jump out of his thin face. It was mostly Marty's job to take care of him, but he was jumpy like he didn't trust him. He would nod when Marty brought food but didn't say thank you. Mrs. Spencer had Marty take him a pail of water with washcloth and soap so he could wash himself. She also found a clean shirt and pants so she could wash the clothes he was wearing. The pants he wore were mud-caked around the bottoms of the legs, and his shirt was torn and stained. When Marty came back to get the pail and his dirty clothes, Joseph was sitting in the sunlight with his shirt off. He grabbed the shirt Marty gave him and started to put it on. But before he could get it on, Marty saw his bare back. It was covered with long, ugly scars that looked like crooked wooden fences.

"Did …?" he started to say "the man who owned you" but caught himself. He thought Joseph might not like that. So, then he asked, "Did someone on the plantation hit you on your back?"

He nodded, and then said, "The massah'. I didn't work hard 'nuff." That was the most words Marty had heard him say.

"He. he shouldn't have done that."

Joseph tucked his chin but didn't say anything.

Marty picked up the stuff, choking back tears. Later, he told his family. Mr. Spencer said, "That's one of the reasons we help."

Another time, Joseph told him, "Baby. I gonna have a baby." He pooched out his stomach, and he smiled for the first time.

Marty didn't understand what he meant. Men don't have babies. He figured it must be something good because he had a half-smile on his face. Marty said, "Good."

Early on a Sunday evening, the Spencer family went to a church social. Mr. Spencer told Joseph they'd be gone and that slave hunters had been seen in the area. Bone would guard the place. He'd be sure to bark if someone came around.

When they came home, Marty went to the attic. Joseph was gone. The blankets he'd used were under a floorboard. He scrambled down the ladder to tell his parents. His father and Ed came up and opened the door of the hidden closet. They found Joseph huddling in the corner.

"I heard 'em. The dog barked. They come through the porch downstairs. They come up here, but I kept real quiet and they went away," he said.

Marty had removed his dishes and the chamber pot before he left for the social. He hated taking care of the chamber pot and forgot to take it back to the attic. That turned out to be good because if the intruders had seen those things, they would have suspected they'd been keeping a fugitive.

Bone? Where was Bone? They found him lying in a corner of the barn. He whimpered when he saw them. His leg was hurt. He tried to get up and walk toward them, but he was limping and shivering.

"They hurt my dog!" Marty was so mad he could spit.

Mr. Spencer said they probably kicked him or hit him with something hard.

He and Ed looked at the back-porch door. The latch was broken. After the men entered the porch, they'd pried open the kitchen window that looked out onto the porch.

Mr. Spencer was angry. "They're gettin' mighty bold—and mean—hurtin' our dog," he said. "Breakin' into a house is a crime. I'm goin' to report it to the sheriff."

The next day, Joseph was taken away in the wagon with the false bottom. "He was a cagey one," Luke Spencer said.

Ed was put to work making the house harder to break into. Mr. Spencer changed his mind about reporting the break-in. Nothing had been stolen, and it might be hard to explain how he knew someone had broken in, if all he could say was that the lock on the porch door was broken. He didn't want to arouse suspicions that slave hunters might be looking for fugitives.

Lena

In the middle of April, the attic was uncomfortably warm during the day, but its next occupant didn't seem to mind. Her name was Lena. She was a little younger than Joseph. The family guessed she was in her late teens. Mrs. Spencer said she would see to her.

Ed managed to get the window unstuck so it could be opened and she could feel a breeze. Lena liked to curl up in the blankets that hadn't been washed since Joseph was there. Mrs. Spencer said that one day she held a blanket to her nose and inhaled its scent. She thought it sounded like she said "Joseph." She looked happy. Mrs. Spencer figured she could smell Joseph's scent and that she and Joseph were a couple that had been separated, or maybe a brother and sister.

Lena always refused breakfast, though she would eat later in the day.

After she'd been there a few days, Marty heard his mother say to his father, "I think she's pregnant. I think she doesn't eat in the morning because she has morning sickness. Luke, you should talk to Gardner about getting her on the road as soon as possible. If she's pregnant, the trip will be harder on her the longer we wait. And another thing, don't even think about trying to fit her into the bottom of that wagon."

Marty put two plus two together. She and Joseph must be man and wife. He told his mother what Joseph had said to him about having a baby, and she said, "I knew it! I don't know how they got separated on their road to freedom."

Lena was spirited away in a wagon at night, dressed in one of Mrs. Spencer's outfits. Marty said a prayer asking that she and Joseph would be together again when her baby came into the world and that they would be happy—and free.

Uncle Tom's Cabin

On a frigid February evening, the family hunkered down around the fireplace to listen to Amy read *Uncle Tom's Cabin*.

The book began with two men bargaining over a slave transaction. One was Mr. Shelby, a plantation owner in Kentucky. The other was a slave trader called Haley. Mr. Shelby owed money to Haley. Though Mr. Shelby didn't want to sell Uncle Tom, a trusted, valuable slave, he felt he must.in order to save his plantation. He tried to convince Haley that Uncle Tom alone would be enough to settle the debt.

He said, "Why, the fact is, Haley, Tom is an uncommon fellow; he is certainly worth that sum anywhere—steady, honest, capable, manages my whole farm like a clock."

Haley wasn't persuaded.

He wanted two slaves. He wanted a pretty woman named Eliza. Mr. Shelby doesn't want to sell Eliza because she is valued by his wife. Then, Eliza's young son Harry entered the room, and Mr. Shelby asked him to imitate some people. They both laughed at his imitations. Haley liked Harry and said he would take him instead of Eliza. Mr. Shelby was reluctant to sell Harry, but he finally agreed. Eliza overheard part of the conversation. She was terribly upset and told Mrs. Shelby, a good Christian woman who treats her slaves well. Mrs. Shelby told Eliza that wouldn't happen. She said, "I would as soon have one of my children sold."

After Amy read the first chapter, the family talked about it. Marty said he liked the way the author described Haley, the slave trader. He asked Amy to read it again. Haley was not a gentleman. He was "a short, thick-set man, with coarse, common-place features, and that swaggering air of pretension which marks a low man who is trying to elbow his way upward in the world. He was much over-dressed, in a gaudy vest of many colors, a blue neckerchief, bedropped gayly with yellow spots, and arranged with a flaunting tie... His hands, large and coarse, were bedecked with rings; and he wore a heavy gold watch-chain…"

Amy said Haley, the slave trader uses degrading language to describe Negroes.

"It is demeaning, and I will not read it aloud, even if Harriet Beecher Stowe uses it in dialog to portray characters in a realistic way."

The part about the young slave boy who Mr. Shelby, his owner, called Jim Crow, made Marty feel twitchy. Was it supposed to be funny when he imitated older black men like Mr. Shelby asked him to? It didn't make him laugh. Amy said it was shameful to ask the boy to make fun of his black elders for the white men.

Marty could see this was good writing—a different type of writing than Reverend Rankin's letters—but really good. He wished he could read more good writing in school.

"Why does Mr. Shelby call Harry 'Jim Crow'?" Ed asked.

Amy said, "My friend Harriet told me that there is a white actor who performs in black face. That means he smears black stuff on his face and acts like a Negro. What he does really is make fun of Negroes."

"Another thing about Jim Crow. He was called a quadroon. What does that mean?" Marty asked—although he thought he already knew.

Mrs. Spencer looked down at her lap. Ed and Amy looked at their father. He looked straight at Marty and said, "It means that he has mixed blood, both white and black."

"Like Aron?"

"Yes, like Aron," he answered.

"Is a quadroon like a mulatto? Amy told me once that Aron was a mulatto."

"Yes, they are similar," his father said.

Marty wanted to ask more questions, but he could see that it was not an easy thing for anyone to talk about. He figured it was one of those things that he would learn more about as he got older.

The Message of Roses

One October day when Marty walked into the barn where Ed and his father were pitching hay for the livestock, he could swear he heard his father say, "There are two roses in the window today." When they saw him, they stopped their conversation.

His father asked, "How was school today, Marty?" He grinned, and then added, "Did you get along okay with Mr. Pitts?"

"Yes, 'course I did."

"I heard today that Mr. Pitts is going to resign. He says teaching doesn't pay him enough money to support his family."

"Do you know who the new teacher will be?"

"No, not yet."

Roses in a window? That was something a woman would be concerned with. He must not have heard right.

That night, Bone was lying in his usual place at the foot of Marty's bed. He began to stir and growl. Marty was groggy, but he got up and went to the window to see if there was anything outside that might be making him growl.

There was a full moon, and he could see well. The buggy appeared with Ed driving. Then his father came to the gate and opened it. Before Ed drove the horses through, his father patted him on the back and seemed to be talking to him.

What was going on? First, roses in a window. Now this. He didn't think he would be able to fall asleep again.

He tossed and turned but finally dozed off. He dreamed of roses in a window and slept late. His mother had to wake him up for school. Hurriedly, he put some water in the basin and splashed it on his face. He started to grab a biscuit to eat while he ran to school, but his mother said to sit and eat some oatmeal.

He was afraid Mr. Pitts would make him stay after school for being late, but Mr. Pitts just frowned and told him to take his seat.

All day, his mind wasn't on his lessons. He kept thinking about the night before—what he'd seen from the window in his room. Where was Ed going late at night? What were he and his father talking about? Should he ask them what it was all about, or just keep quiet? He finally decided to wait. He would just watch them. Maybe he'll find out eventually.

∞∞∞∞

At Christmas time, the Spencers attended a party at the home of Reverend William Hanby and his family in Westerville, a town nearby Worthington. Reverend Hanby was a minister of the United Brethren Church and a co-founder of Otterbein University, the school Amy wanted to attend. Reverend Hanby's son, Benjamin, was a musician and a composer. At the gathering, he played the piano, and everyone sang Christmas carols. They served some delicious sugar cookies and hot chocolate.

When the visit was over, the Spencers walked through the parlor on the way out. Marty noticed something that made him stop in his tracks. There was a vase that held three red roses! Not two roses as his father said to Ed, but three. Could that have some connection to what he overheard them talking about? It didn't seem likely, but—

Mrs. Spencer asked the children, "Did you have a good time?"

They all said yes.

Then, the devil got a hold of Marty. He said, "I thought the roses in the vase by the window were pretty."

Ed jerked his head at him. "What do you know about roses, little brother?"

"Oh, not much—just that they're pretty."

Ed looked at him as though to say, "I think you're trying to pull my leg."

And he was—but he let it go.

Ed must have mentioned it to their father. Maybe he said something like "I think maybe Marty overheard us in the barn when we were talking about roses in the window."

A few days later, Mr. Spencer told the children that Reverend Hanby was an abolitionist who hid slaves in his barn. He said that Ed had helped him take some runaway slaves to Delaware County a couple of times. The roses in the window were a message telling how many slaves needed help. Marty couldn't believe it—a Reverend breaking the law! But he knew he was doing it because he thought it was the right thing to do, even if it was breaking the law.

Their father said, "Reverend Hanby once was himself a sort of slave. When he was a boy, his father died. He and his mother were extremely poor, and she indentured him to a cruel man, actually a Quaker. Now, I know we talked about Levi Coffin and most Quakers being kind and helping slaves, but this man was a different breed. Reverend Hanby finally ran away from him, but that experience made him feel 'specially sorry for other people in bondage. Of course, as I've said before, I can't stress enough that we do not talk about this outside of this family."

"I saw you—you and Ed—one night out my window. Ed took the buggy," said Marty.

"Yes, Ed helped out Reverend Hanby with some runaways. You got sharp eyes and ears, Marty, but keep your mouth closed."

"Could I help, too? I want to help."

"Not now. We'll see. Maybe there'll be a way later on."

1856

Politics and Conflict

Early in the winter of 1856, Luke Spencer fell into the habit of joining a group of companionable men at Isaac's General Store in the afternoon. The men sat around a potbelly stove and chewed the fat. They occupied two comfortable rockers or straight-backed chairs; the ones who got there first got the rockers. A couple of them were tobacco chewers and, for them, there was a spittoon. There were four regulars, including the store owner, Isaac. Walt was a retired farmer; Perry, a retired tool and die maker. Otto, an itinerant peddler joined them from time to time. To them, Luke Spencer was "Spence."

Though the men had known each other by sight or by casual connection, they had not really been friends before they started their gatherings in Isaac's store. Isaac was the hub. He was talkative and without even realizing what he was doing, selected the men as compatible company and good conversationalists for slow afternoons. They had, of course, all been his customers and still were.

Occasionally, there were two other visitors, Marty Spencer and Bone. Marty liked to listen to the men talk, and they were indulgent with him. Isaac usually found a licorice stick or another treat for him. He told Marty that he should call him Isaac, not Mr. Johnson, but Marty didn't feel right doing that, so he usually avoided addressing him at all. Isaac allowed him to bring Bone to the store, and Bone was well-behaved, sleeping near Marty's feet. Occasionally, he snored, and the men thought that was funny.

When the bell on the door rang, Isaac would get up and amble to the front to wait on the customer. Isaac was a widower in his late sixties, and many people in the community thought he kept the store operating just because he liked contact with his customers. He ingratiated himself with women who were good cooks, so he would get invited to dinner. Virginia Spencer was one of those women who took pity on him, and, once a month or so, Spence would invite him to dinner.

All the men had abolitionist sympathies but were not regularly involved in helping runaways. In that respect, Luke Spencer was more involved than the others, and that activity was only recently. Isaac once hid an escapee in a barrel in the back of the store and piled merchandise on top of him. Walt had helped Ozem Gardner once by hauling a load of hay with a hollowed-out place that held a young Negro woman. Perry had provided food and drink for runaways and let a man hide under a tarp overnight in his shop once. Otto had given two runaways a ride in his wagon along a country road. None of them talked about these activities. It was not so much that they distrusted each other. They just didn't think they should talk about them. And, of course, they were wary because of the Fugitive Slave Act. Their main topic was local happenings and gossip, and more seriously, the state of the Union. On the latter topic, the issue of slavery was an important part of their concerns and discussions.

They talked about the scandalous tragedy of Margaret Garner, a Kentucky slave woman who escaped with her family in a sleigh across the frozen Ohio River near Cincinnati. She was pursued by slaveholders. When cornered, she slashed the throat of her two-year-old daughter and lashed out at her other three children because she didn't want them raised in slavery.

Ohio's Governor Chase wanted Garner returned to the Cincinnati area to stand trial, but she was returned to her owner, who then sold her and her family to a slaveholder in Louisiana.

They talked about current politics. They talked about the clashes between slavers and abolitionists, about whether Southern states would secede, and if so, which ones. And what would the country be like with two governments?

Otto always had something exciting to report when he returned from his travels. Some of his tales, his friends found incredulous, but they listened without questioning him. Once, he told them that he had been captured by a band of renegade Indians. They took him to their camp, where they drank several bottles of whiskey that he had in his carriage. When they passed out, he was able to escape. Yes, Otto certainly added color to their lives.

His latest tales were realistic. He had been to "bleeding Kansas" where he said things were "hotter 'n hell." Slavers and abolitionists were in violent conflict that was largely a fallout from the Kansas-Nebraska Act, enacted by Congress two years ago. The Ohio friends were aware of the act, as were most people who were concerned about the possible expansion of slavery in free states. The Act allowed for the new territories of Kansas and Nebraska to decide by popular vote whether they wanted to be slave states or free states. Since 1820, the Missouri Compromise had been in effect. It stipulated that slavery would be banned in the lands included in the former Louisiana Purchase that ran north of an imaginary line running along Missouri's border. The Kansas-Nebraska Act in effect negated the Missouri Compromise, opening the door for the expansion of slavery in free states.

In May, Otto reported that Missouri pro-slavers were crossing the state line and voting illegally in Kansas, angering "Free Staters." Pro-slavers sacked and burned the town of Lawrence, Kansas, a stronghold of abolitionists. Otto said he had been showing his wares to a woman in Lawrence when the attack began, and he had to get out of town pronto. Then, in retaliation, a group of abolitionists led by a man named John Brown attacked and killed several pro-slavers.

Another shocker that was fodder for conversations among the friends was an incident in Congress. After Senator Charles Sumner of Massachusetts made a speech ridiculing slaveowners, Congressman Preston Brooks of South Carolina beat Sumner nearly to death with his cane, leaving him incapacitated. That such a thing could happen in the hallowed halls of Congress left them dumfounded.

Increasingly, the friends felt that the nation was moving in the wrong direction. Although none of them had been particularly political before, they made a group decision to support the fledgling Republican Party that had been formed a year or so ago. The Republicans opposed the repeal of the Missouri Compromise and the extension of slavery into the free territories. John C. Fremont, nicknamed the "Pathfinder" because of his activities as an explorer and mapmaker of the West, was its candidate. Their slogan was "Free Soil, Free Labor, Free Speech, Free Men, and Fremont." A banner showed Fremont riding a rearing horse. He had a rifle slung over his shoulder and waved his hat in the air.

"There's gonna be a reckoning. There's just too much dark stuff goin' on."

Marty usually listened quietly to the men's conversation, but Isaac's remark prompted him to ask, "Isaac…?"

"Yes. Son?"

"What-what do you think will happen?"

"War, son. I think there'll be a war."

It was an answer Marty didn't expect. His was a tranquil, protected existence. He couldn't imagine a war in which a lot of people would kill and be killed. His father frowned. He thought Isaac's answer was too severe.

Later, Marty asked his father if he thought there would be a war. His father said he thought there would be skirmishes, outbreaks of violence in parts of the country, but probably not a full-scale war.

The Democratic Party nominated James Buchanan and supported letting the people vote for or against slavery in Kansas and free states. They said that the Republican Party would be so divisive it would cause a Civil War. The Know-Nothing Party, who nominated Millard Fillmore, seemed to live up to its name and left slavery alone but was anti-Catholic and anti-immigration. James Buchanan won.

The friends were disappointed but not surprised. Isaac said, "Mark my words."

Routes to Freedom

One night, Ed asked his father about the routes that runaways take through Ohio to get to Canada. Ed liked to know details. Mr. Spencer got an Ohio map and showed the family a route that they might take. "Okay, I'll try to give you the big picture of how runaways might make their way through Ohio to Canada."

He said there were several routes they might take, depending on where they cross the Ohio River, but one might be at Portsmouth, Ohio, just across the river from Kentucky. From there, they might get help from a free slave or a white abolitionist who would start them on their journey. They'd take the route north through several counties—Pike, Ross, and Pickaway.

"When they reach the town of Circleville in Pickaway County, they'll be only about 20 miles from Columbus, in Franklin County. We live in northern Franklin County. In Columbus, there are several Underground Railroad stations. One I know of is called Kelton House. I believe that a free slave named Washington, who owns several teams and wagons, often helps them. He might take them to the Clinton Chapel on High Street to be held for a short time.

"The slaves are often picked up by Ansel Matoon. I think I mentioned him to you before. Ansel is a blacksmith and wagon maker, and he is frequently out and about because of his business. He'd probably leave the slaves on Gardner's land in the secret shelter on the side of the creek bank. Gardner might take care of them a while—or maybe ask us for help sometimes.

"From there, they might go to Reverend Hanby's barn where someone else would help them get to Delaware County, just north of us. They might stop at a station operated by a man named Patterson near Alum Creek.

"After that, they travel through several northern counties until they reach Sandusky, on Lake Erie. There, they find safe boat passage across Lake Erie to Canada."

Now, the Spencer kids could picture in their minds how slaves traveled through Ohio. Marty was surprised at how much clearer this made things for him.

"Could we go see Mr. Gardner's shelter?" he asked.

"We'll do that sometime when I'm sure there are no slave hunters watching."

But he had more questions—always questions. He wondered how slaves found their way north when they were in a strange place, lost in the woods maybe, with no one around to help them.

Mr. Spencer said they know how to follow the North Star, and they also follow streams and look at moss on trees. "Moss likes shade, so it grows thicker on the north side of trees."

He sat for a while, then said, "Most slaves aren't taught to read or write because that might make them uppity and improve themselves and make them want their freedom. So, they are at a disadvantage. For instance, they can't read signs that might help them find their way."

Ed said, "I've been able to see the Big Dipper in the sky. Is the North Star part of that?"

"Not exactly, but you can find the North Star by using the Big Dipper. If you drew a straight line from the outermost stars in the bowl of the Big Dipper, you'd locate the North Star. It touches the handle of the Little Dipper. We'll look for it sometime when the weather is good."

That night, Marty had a hard time going to sleep. He lay thinking about all the things he'd learned from his father about the Underground Railroad. It was interesting and pretty exciting stuff—hidden runaways, slave hunters, a U.S. Marshal. He wished school were that interesting.

One thing he did learn in school was about the Northwest Ordinance of 1797 that formed the Northwest Territory, a territory created out of land gained from Great Britain. It established a way for new states to be admitted to the Union. Ohio was a part of that Territory and became a state in 1803. One especially important part of the Northwest Ordinance was that the states in the Territory would be free states. That meant slavery was not allowed. He thought that was good, and he was proud to live in a free state.

Repression and Rebellion

On another night, Mr. Spencer told them about some Ohio laws that were not good for Negroes. The Black Laws passed in the early 1800's required them to post a $500 bond just so they could live in Ohio. Anyone who hired them without what is called a "certificate of freedom" could be fined and required to make restitution to the slave's owner. What's more Black people couldn't testify in court in trials in which whites were involved. Ohio might be a free state, but it didn't seem to welcome Black people.

The kids wanted him to tell them more about free Blacks in their area. Were there many of them?

"One prominent man is Reverend James Poindexter. He leads the antislavery Second Baptist Church. He preaches openly against slavery. He owns a barber shop and is involved in the city council. He's a man whose looks will catch your attention. It is said that his mother was a black Cherokee and his father white. All these lines seem to blend in his face, and he has a mane of white hair.

"Another Black man is John Ward who owns a moving company. And another man named Washington. Now, it's hard to know how much some of these men are involved in helping runaways—but it's a good bet to assume that they do. They must be careful and secretive because of the Fugitive Slave Law.

"Now, in Ripley where Seth lives, there's a man named John Parker, a former slave who managed to buy his freedom and start a successful business. It is said that he is very bold and goes into slave territory to lead slaves to freedom.

"Another thing about free Blacks— Well, it's not so much a problem around here. but in other places like the Cincinnati area, they have been captured and sold to southern whites. It can become violent. One of the worst stories I heard was about a man who was the child of a white slave owner and one of his slaves. By appearance, one couldn't tell that he had Negro blood, and he himself did not know. He was educated and eventually got a good job, married a white woman, and had children, maybe four or five. Then, his father died, and the people who inherited the property and wealth of the father said that the son was the property of the estate. They hired slave hunters to hunt him down. They broke into his home, bound him, and took him to the plantation. His wife was so shocked that it ruined her health, and she died. When he was finally able to gain his freedom, he learned of his wife's death, and he himself soon died."

"What happened to the children?" Amy asked.

"That I don't know. I believe that is a story told by Levi Coffin, the President of the Underground Railroad."

"How can they do that?" Amy asked. Marty could hear tears in her voice. He felt that way, too.

"Amy, it's greed and meanness and having no respect for Blacks as human beings." Her father reached over and patted her hand.

They sat in silence for a while. Then, Amy asked her father, "Do slaves sometimes fight back … against the oppression?"

Marty was impressed by the word 'oppression.' He liked the sound of it and felt proud that his sister was so smart.

"Oh, yes," her father answered. "There was a bloody rebellion led by a slave named Nat Turner in Virginia in 1830 or 1831, I believe. I'm not sure you really want to hear about it…"

But having heard that much, they all agreed that they were strong enough to hear the rest.

"Turner and a group of slaves killed over fifty white people—men, women, and children. The whites immediately formed militias and captured and executed around fifty Negroes accused of being party to the attack. Nat Turner himself was at bay for a couple of months, but then, he was captured and hanged. Supposedly, he said he had a vision from God that told him to slay his enemies.

"Whites were terrified and wanted revenge. It is said that they also killed many innocent Negroes who had no part in the murders. Then, they passed all kinds of laws to prevent such uprisings. For instance, a law forbade the education of slaves. See, Nat Turner knew how to read and write and was said to be highly intelligent. He was also religious and preached to groups of slaves, so laws were passed limiting rights to assemble in groups."

"Did the slaves have firearms?" asked Ed.

"No, I believe they used axes, knives, and hatchets."

The Spencer children sat in stunned silence about the horrific story their father had told them.

Finally, Ed spoke up. "It's awful beyond words, but I can sort of understand what drove them…"

At first, Amy and Marty were taken aback at their brother's comment, but then they both nodded in agreement.

1857

More School Troubles

Marty got in trouble at school again, but thank goodness, he didn't have to deal with Mr. Pitts. Miss Fields was a lot better. Amy was glad that he had a woman teacher. She asked him lots of questions about Miss Fields.

The trouble started during lunch break when Marty was with three other guys just walking around a bit. One of them, a guy named Joe, started talking about Black people who moved close to his neighborhood. He mimicked a Negro dialect to make fun of them.

Joe kept using language like Haley, the slave trader in *Uncle Tom's Cabin* used and Amy refused to read aloud. Marty got agitated and started walking away. He muttered, "You shouldn't talk that way." It just slipped out before he thought about it."

Joe whipped his head around and stared at him. "What'd you say?"

"N-Nothin'."

"You said somethin' What was it?" he demanded.

"I-I just said, "We don't talk that way about Black people in my family.""

He grabbed Marty's arm and twisted it. "Well, we're not highfalutin'. We'll talk the way we want to, won't we guys?"

Marty pulled his arm away and shoved him, and first thing you know, they were fighting and the other guys, who were more Joe's friends than Marty's, started egging him on. Miss Fields came running outside and yelled at them to stop. She stepped between them to separate them. She demanded that they tell her what they were fighting about.

She said, "Martin is right. We should be more respectful in the way we talk about Blacks. I don't want to see any more fighting over this. Understand?"

But Joe was mad and scowled at Marty every time they happened to look at each other for the rest of the day. He didn't like that Miss Fields took Marty's part.

Marty could hardly wait for the day to end. When Miss Fields dismissed them, he tore out the door and ran most of the way home, which was almost a mile from school.

The next day, his enemies had a plan. When school let out, they got ahead of him and waited to attack him after he came around a bend in the road. They started pelting him with snowballs. It had snowed all day, and it was hard to run, and he had an ache in his bad leg. It was one against three. Marty was getting killed. He walked as fast as he could, but they caught up with him and knocked him down. They dumped snow on his face, and one of them kicked his bad leg.

"Is this being disrespectful? You goin' to be a baby and tattle to the teacher?" Joe jeered.

But then suddenly they stopped and started to run back toward the school.

Marty couldn't believe it when Ed rode up on Big Man. Big Man was their horse that they mainly used for pulling their buggy. He was strong, but gentle and friendly. Marty stood up unsteadily and brushed the snow off as best he could. He put his face by Big Man's head and nuzzled him.

Ed reached down and pulled him up behind him on Big Man. The snow started coming down harder, and Marty thought it was a beautiful thing riding behind his brother on Big Man through the snow. Snowflakes fell on his face and tongue, and he felt safe and happy.

"What was happening there, little brother? Those guys looked like they were trying to beat you up. It's a good thing I decided to come for you since it's snowed so much."

"Yeah, that's pretty much what they were trying to do"

"What … Why would they do that?"

Marty told him.

"Big Man and I will come and get you after school until all this blows over. If they try to do that again, they'll have me to answer to."

After a few minutes, Ed said, "Now, you've seen firsthand how this race stuff riles people up. You'll be more careful from now on."

The snow continued the next day. Mr. Spencer pronounced it very nearly a blizzard. Marty stayed home for the next two days. Amy was now attending Otterbein, and her classes were also canceled.

Restless, Marty hung around Amy. She showed him a list of courses she was taking. Her program was called a Preparatory Course, which included Reading, using McGuffey's Fifth Reader; English Grammar; English Analysis; Geography; Arithmetic; History; Watts on the Mind; and the English Bible, one lesson per week.

"What is 'Watts on the Mind'?" he asked.

She said it contained lessons on how to improve your thinking.

He leafed through the *McGuffey Reader*. It stressed "elocution," a word he did not know. Amy said it had to do with clear pronunciation and "articulation," another word Marty did not know. But he understood it was about talking and pronouncing words properly. He thought this must be why Amy liked to read poems and stories aloud to the family.

Marty pestered Amy to tell him what happened in *Uncle Tom's Cabin*. He wanted to know what happened to Eliza and Harry. Did they see George Harris again? And what about Uncle Tom? What happened to him? Was he sold to a master who treated him well? Amy told him he'd have to wait to hear what happened when she read more of it to the family. He thought about stealing the book from her room and reading it himself, but he felt too restless to do that.

Uncle Tom's Cabin

Amy read two more chapters of *Uncle Tom's Cabin*. Marty almost couldn't bear to listen to it. He thought the whole book was going to be sad, but as Amy said, it was meant to make people understand the evils of slavery.

Chapter Two was about George Harris, Eliza's husband. He was a slave on a different plantation. His owner put him to work in a factory where he did really good work and even invented a machine for cleaning hemp, which the author wrote "displayed quite as much mechanical genius as Whitney's cotton gin." He was a favorite in the factory, but he was under the control of "a vulgar, narrow-minded, tyrannical master," who couldn't stand the fact that his slave got so much attention. He took him away from the factory and put him to work doing the meanest, dirtiest work on the farm.

George came to Eliza and told her his owner wouldn't allow him to keep a pet dog. He ordered him to tie a stone around his neck and throw him in the pond. When George refused to do that, the owner and his son did it. George got a flogging because he wouldn't kill his dog.

Marty looked down at Bone snoozing peacefully at his feet. He remembered how his family came home and found him hurt after slave hunters broke into their house. He still had a slight limp—so he was kind of like him with his limp. He wished with all his heart that it didn't happen to Bone. How could people drown a dog by tying stones around his neck?

And to top all the bad things that happened to George, he was told that he wouldn't be able to keep Eliza for a wife anymore. If he didn't settle down with another slave woman, he would be sold down the river.

George told Eliza he couldn't take it anymore. He was running away to Canada.

And when Amy finished reading, Marty said, "I can't take any more of these terrible stories. I'm not going to listen to this book anymore."

Amy said, "But Marty there are some good people in the book. You'll see…"

"I don't care," he said. "It's just too much meanness."

Mr. Spencer said, "Marty, I know it's hard to listen to, but this book is based on incidents that could happen in real life. Stories like these … They are why I've allowed people to hide in our basement and attic. So, Marty, I know how you feel, but I hope you will listen… We have to be tough."

Marty couldn't get the story of George Harris out of his head. He thought about the words of Reverend Rankin—that Negroes are seldom given any chance for improvement or encouragement of genius.

"Darling Nellie Gray"

The Spencer family was invited to Hanby's home for a Fourth of July party. Mr. Gardner's family and a dozen or so people were there. Ed said it was a party mostly for abolitionists. Benjamin Hanby, Reverend Hanby's son, played the piano and sang a special song he wrote:

> *One night I went to see her, but she's gone the neighbors say*
> *And the white man had bound her with his chain*
> *They have taken her to Georgia for to wear her life away*
> *As she toils in the cotton and the cane.*
>
> *Oh, my poor Nellie Gray, they have taken you away*
> *And I'll never see my darling, anymore*
> *I'm sitting by the river and a weeping all the day*
> *For you've gone from the old Kentucky shore*

Benjamin Hanby explained to the guests that it was written as if the words were spoken by another man, a runaway slave whose sweetheart had been sold South by slave owners. He was broken-hearted and hoped to meet her again in heaven. It was based on the story of a real runaway. Reverend William Hanby had tried to help buy the woman's freedom.

Another sad story! Marty thought. But it seemed to make the rest of his family cheerful because they believed it would become popular and help the abolitionists' cause, just the way *Uncle Tom's Cabin* was bringing to light the evils of slavery.

That evening, the Spencer family sat on a blanket on their lawn and searched for the north star. Ed and Mr. Spencer found it right away. The others took longer, but all had the satisfaction of finding it. It capped off their 4th of July celebration.

Just before they retired, Amy wanted to read the family a poem by John Greenleaf Whittier, who was a Quaker and an abolitionist. It was about a slave mourning her daughter who was sold:

> *Gone, gone--sold and gone,*
> *To the rice-swamp dank and lone,*
> *From Virginia's hills and waters;*
> *Woe is me, my stolen daughters!*

Amy said it was like Benjamin Hanby's song because it was written as though a slave were writing it, and it was about someone who was loved being sold down South.

Uncle Tom's Cabin

Marty was back in his chair again to listen to Amy read *Uncle Tom's Cabin.* She promised him that there would be less meanness this time.

Amy started by saying she would skip some of the parts that use what she calls "Negro dialect." She said that even though Harriet Beecher Stowe wanted to portray Negroes as they really talk, she felt like she'd be making fun of them when she read it aloud, so she would summarize those parts.

Mr. Shelby confessed to his wife that he had sold little Eliza's son Harry and Uncle Tom. Mrs. Shelby was very upset. She had never approved of slavery but thought that if she treated their slaves well, it wouldn't be so bad. Mr. Shelby told her that the slave dealer was a hard man. It had to be done or they would have been in total ruin.

Mrs. Shelby wanted to sell some of her jewelry to help, but Mr. Shelby had already done the deal. She said, "This is God's curse on slavery! —a bitter, bitter, most accursed thing! —a curse to the master and a curse to the slave! I was a fool to think I could make anything good out of such a deadly evil."

Young Master George Shelby, the son, was also unhappy. He liked to go to Uncle Tom's cabin and eat Aunt Chloe's food and be in their company. Aunt Chloe was Uncle Tom's wife. Marty imagined Master George to be about his age. He liked him and Mrs. Shelby. At last, he thought, some white people who are good people.

But the main thing was that Eliza was hiding in a closet next to the Shelby's bedroom and overheard the conversation. Quickly, she decided to take Harry and run away.

Even though everyone was tired, and Amy interrupted her reading with several yawns, the family wanted her to keep reading because they wanted to know if Eliza made it to freedom.

Of course, when Haley, the slave trader, found out Eliza has run away and taken Harry, he was in a rage. He thought maybe Mr. Shelby helped her in some way. Mr. Shelby denied it and promised to help him track Eliza.

When Eliza came to the river, she saw that it was nearly blocked with ice. Her heart sank because she wanted to take the ferry. She went to a house where a kind couple let her and Harry rest. When Haley and the slaves came to the house, a slave named Sam managed to warn her. Eliza grabbed her son and ran to the river. She jumped from one block of ice to another, and she got all the way across. Then, a man directed her to a house where she might get help. Marty thought it was unbelievable how she crossed the river on the ice

Mr. Spencer said that Eliza's escape across the river was based on a real incident. He said, "I believe it was Reverend Rankin who told that story—either him or Levi Coffin."

Ed's Important Announcement

When Amy finished reading, Mr. Spencer said he had an important announcement to make. After the autumn harvest was finished, Ed would be starting something new.

Marty and Amy, who had been tired before, now leaned forward in their chairs eagerly, wondering what their father would say.

"Ed is 18 years old now, and he needs to learn a new trade. He'll be starting an apprenticeship with Uncle Seth to learn furniture making."

"But Uncle Seth lives in Ripley, Ohio," Marty said in a tone of protest. "How can he do that?"

"Ed will have to move to Ripley and live with Uncle Seth."

Both Marty and Amy were stunned. They'd never thought about Ed being old enough to leave the family.

Marty couldn't imagine the family without Ed. He felt like someone had punched him in the chest. He thought about the day Ed had rescued him when his classmates were attacking him in the snow. He remembered how good, how safe, he felt riding behind his brother on Big Boy. He thought about Ed playfully pushing him and Bone down the hill on the sled.

"We'll still see Ed," reassured Mr. Spencer. "He'll come back to visit, and we'll go see him."

Marty was able to hold back his tears until he was in bed. Then, he buried his head under his pillow so no one would hear him and cried himself to sleep.

Other tears were shed in the Spencer household, too. Amy also cried. She remembered Ed making furniture for her basement school when they sheltered Tom and Dora. And she remembered him teaching Bone tricks.

Even Ed had a few tears run down his cheeks because he knew his family would miss him. He'd seen it in their faces when his father told them the news. He was both eager to take the step into adulthood and anxious about leaving the security of his family.

In their parents' bedroom, Mr. Spencer reached to comfort his wife when she choked up. "Marty and Amy are going to miss Ed. Well, we'll all miss him… but it will be especially hard for Marty."

A Delivery Job

In late August, Mr. Spencer agreed to let his children carry out a rescue mission. A fugitive had been picked up from Kelton House in Columbus and brought to Mr. Gardner. Word was out that the man's owner had offered $1,200 for his capture, and slave hunters were out in force.

The plan was to move the man during daytime in the wagon with the false bottom. The wagon would be loaded with fruits and vegetables and driven north to a market in Delaware County. Ed would steer the wagon, and Marty would ride in back. Amy would sit by Ed or maybe be in back with Marty if there was room. Mr. Spencer worried about this plan and was about to change his mind, but they begged him to let them do it. They thought Mr. Gardner was right when he said that three young people were less likely to arouse suspicion.

The three children were game.

The runaway was a slender man who had obligingly climbed into the false bottom and curled himself into a tight ball. Though there was a hot, dry wind that alleviated the August heat, the man could not feel the breeze. Marty knew that there were holes that let him breathe, but, still, he thought the man must be miserable. He worried that he might get overheated and sick.

When they were about halfway to their destination, the two slave hunters that Marty and Tom had met in the ravine that day, the same ones that later came to their house and argued with their father, appeared behind them on horseback.

Marty, facing backward, was the first to notice them. He hissed a warning to Ed and Amy.

Ed said, "Just keep calm. If they come close, don't act nervous like we've got something to hide."

Soon, the men caught up to their wagon and asked Ed if they could buy a watermelon and some corn off the wagon. Ed said, well, he was supposed to deliver all the produce to a market, but he guessed it would be okay to sell one watermelon and a couple ears of corn.

While Ed helped them pick out a watermelon, Marty, who was so scared he had to sit on his hands to keep them from shaking, admired how composed his brother was.

Finishing the transaction, the big guy took notice of Marty and glared at him. Marty half expected him to jerk him off the wagon so he could search it.

"Ain't you that boy we seen in the ravine one day? You was with a dark-skinned boy you said was your cuzzin."

He said "cuzzin" in a way that let him know he didn't believe that story. Marty nodded his head but kept quiet.

"We talked to your pa, and he weren't very cooperative. A marshal come and warned him…" The man smiled meanly, like he enjoyed making Marty squirm.

Ed interrupted, "Look mister, we don't know anything about that. Our daddy is a respectable man … We gotta deliver this produce and get back home before dark." He sounded like his father when he stood up to the men at their house. He sounded like a grownup who was ready to leave the family…

The man scowled but took the watermelon and corn, and they were on our way again. As they pulled away, Marty saw him stab the watermelon. He didn't just cut it—he stabbed it until it fell apart. Marty shivered in the heat.

It wasn't long before the slave hunters were trailing them again. They followed them all the way to Delaware. When they arrived at the market, William Cratty, the owner, asked the Spencer children to help him unload part of the produce. The slave hunters sat on their horses and watched from a distance as they worked, but finally, they moved on. Ed was able to drive the wagon to the back of the market where the perspiring man was glad to escape from the false bottom.

Marty had been scared, but a day or two later, he was itching to do it again. Their father wasn't eager to let them get involved in helping a runaway again, at least, in broad daylight. He said he wasn't sure whether the slave hunters suspected the children of helping a runaway or whether they just wanted to scare them for the heck of it. Either way, it made him uneasy. They might be in danger. But a few days later, he said he thought it would be a good idea for Marty to help Mr. Gardner sell his produce even when there were no fugitives involved. He said people would get used to seeing him around doing innocent work and it would be helpful to Mr. Gardner. Mr. Gardner would even pay him for his help.

1858

A Visitor in Ripley

Marty surveyed the busy scene from a bench above the Ripley port on the Ohio River. The river sparkled in the sunlight. It was a steamy July day, and he felt listless, but he observed that much was being accomplished on the river front.

A steamboat docked and discharged two passengers down the gangway. Workers unloaded their wares from two wagons onto flatboats, probably the products of a Ripley boatyard; others prepared to load materials onto the steamboat. Several other people walked to and fro, hither and yon, just hanging out or maybe engaged in some activity, the purpose of which was not discernible to an inexperienced observer.

Across the river, Marty could make out children on a pier, viewing the same scene from a different angle in the completely different state of Kentucky. He found himself wondering if those children's parents owned slaves who cooked their food, cleaned their houses, and took care of those very children. If those children's parents were slave owners, were they kind to their slaves or mean to them? He thought about the Kentucky slave woman Margaret Garner he'd learned about from his father and friends. She was a woman who killed her own child because she didn't want her to be raised in slavery the way she herself had been.

It seemed strange to him that a river could separate two states often at odds with each other over the issue of slavery. The river benefited both states in commerce but was the means of escape for slaves seeking freedom and clashes between the people hunting them and the people helping them.

Lest the normal daytime activity belie what happened at night, Marty had only to turn around and look upwards to see a concrete reminder of the explosive issue of slavery. There on the hill was Reverend Rankin's house, the house of the man he had learned about from his father—whose articulate words he had read in the letters written to a brother on the inhumaneness of slavery as an institution. The house where a lamp burned in the window as a beacon to runaways at night.

A bearded, garrulous old man joined him on the bench. He wore overalls and, despite the heat, a worn buckskin jacket. Once before, he'd come to sit with Marty and introduced himself as Dan. "Some people call me Daniel Boone 'cause I wear buckskin." He'd took it upon himself to educate the lad about Ripley and the Ohio River, and sometimes, he told tales about fighting "Injuns." Marty was skeptical beyond his years about these tales, but he played along and listened attentively.

"The great Ohio! It starts in Pittsburgh at the confluence of the Allegheny and Monongahela rivers. Monongahela, now that's a mouthful—Injun name, I guess. Confluence means 'coming together.' Did you know that? It flows all the way down to Cairo, a city on the southern tip of the state of Illinois. Bet you didn't know that, boy."

Marty shook his head no. "What happens to the river in Cairo?"

He thought he remembered from a geography lesson that it flowed into the Mississippi River but asked the question to humor Dan, who reminded him of his father's friends who gathered at the back of the general store in Worthington.

"Why, it flows right into the mighty Mississippi. The Ohio might not be as mighty as the mighty Miss', but it's a great river. A good river. In fact, that's what its name means, 'good river.'

"Just look at what happens. Pork comes from the slaughterhouse, flour comes from the mills, lumber from the sawmills, iron from the foundries—all of it transported on the Ohio to help people make a living and build this nation… And let's not forget the Ripley boatyards that give us the means to do it…

"Somthin' else you prob'ly don't know much about … The river pretty much separates slave states and free states … Just look over there and see Kentuck'. People are allowed to own black men, slaves … but not here in Ohio."

∞∞∞

As Marty watched the town of Ripley and its inhabitants from what he had come to think of as his bench, he felt he had a secret cache of knowledge about the place. This came from the many times his father, Spence, had held forth about tales of abolitionists in the evenings at home. He didn't let on to Dan how much he knew. He wasn't sure whether Dan's sympathies lay with abolitionists.

Marty hadn't yet seen John Rankin. Possibly he might have seen one of the Rankin sons. If he'd seen them, he wouldn't have known it because he'd never met them or had someone identify them to him. But he'd identified another man who seemed to have just stepped out of one of his father's stories.

He was the former slave named John Parker who owned a successful iron foundry that was near his home on the bank of the river. Occasionally, Parker would walk through town on his way to the port, presumably on business. He always walked in the middle of the street. The handle of a pistol was evident in a holster on his right hip.

"He's a strutter, aint't he?" Dan asked, though it wasn't really a question. "Know why he always walks down the middle of the street?"

Marty shook his head no.

"Well, it's said a lot of slave hunters would like to capture him. He's afeared someone might jump on him from an alley. There's supposed to be quite a price on his head in Kentucky, maybe other southern states, too. Could be a thousand dollars or more."

"You mean they want to return him to a slave owner?"

"Nah, he's a free man, bought his freedom, I understand. He'd prob'ly be thrown in the clinker—or hanged. They say he's helped a lot of runaway slaves cross the river."

"Really?" Marty asked in what he hoped was a surprised voice. "How does he do that?"

"Well, 'course it's done at night. I don't know how he does it, but you can tell from watchin' him that he's a sneaky one. Just watchin' him reminds me of an Injun trackin' somebody or somethin' in the woods."

Marty understood what Dan meant. John Parker was a tall, muscular man with a medium skin tone. He gave the impression of power but was catlike, graceful in his movements. Arms, torso, legs, and feet seem to flow effortlessly in sync. He also seemed preternaturally alert to his surroundings without being too obvious about it.

Ripley had taken on mythical proportions in Marty's imagination. He longed to have contact with its secrets—what happened in Ripley in the dark of night. He knew he'd have to be careful. His brother Ed and Uncle Seth had warned him that there could be explosive flare-ups between slave hunters and abolitionists in Ripley. Well, he'd known that. Hadn't Spence—he'd taken to thinking of his father as Spence since he'd come to Ripley—warned him and Amy and Ed many times not to talk about abolition and hiding slaves back home in Worthington? And here by the river where slaves were nearer the places they were escaping from and the town practically swarming with slave hunters, well, he knew to be doubly careful. He often thought about the story of the Rankin house being practically under siege by slave hunters, though it was hard to imagine when it seemed so tranquil in the daytime.

But Marty was just a visitor to Ripley, not an inhabitant. His parents had permitted him to hitch a ride with Otto, the peddler, who was going to the Cincinnati area. Otto delivered him to Uncle Seth's place of business and then went on his way to Cincinnati, some fifty miles away. Marty had been staying with his uncle and Ed for three weeks, but soon, they would be leaving. He and Ed would be taking off. Uncle Seth was going to let them borrow his horse and buggy. They would be going home to Worthington. Ed would stay to help with the fall harvest, and then he would come back to continue his apprenticeship with Uncle Seth. Marty would stay in Worthington.

Return to Worthington

Bone was beside himself to see Ed and Marty. He ran around them in joyous circles.

"Roll over, Bone," Ed commanded, and he immediately obeyed.

"Good boy, you remembered!"

He patted him on the head, and Bone tried to lick his hand. Then, Bone immediately ran to Marty, as if he didn't want to leave him out of things.

In the short time they'd been gone, they could see changes in their father. He said his "rheumatiz" was acting up. His fingers were stiff and painful, and his right index finger was curved outwardly at a funny angle. He said his knees also bothered him some. Their mother said he had a hard time getting going in the morning. He'd always been slender but with a sinewy strength. Now, it seemed his body had lost some of its solidity. Mr. Spencer, who was in his late sixties, had married late and was ten years his wife's senior, and the age difference showed more now. Though her hair was a little grayer, Mrs. Spencer's pleasant, slightly plump face showed few lines, and she was sprightly in her movements.

Amy chatted away about a female writer she had discovered. Her name was Frances Dana Gage. She was not only a writer. She was also a public speaker and active in working for three causes—abolitionism, women's rights, and temperance. Amy wasn't much interested in temperance, but, of course, she considered herself an abolitionist, and her eyes had a special sparkle when she talked about women's rights.

Frances Dana Gage, it seemed was a dynamo. She was a poet, a novelist, and a newspaper columnist, contributing articles regularly to the *Ohio Cultivator*, an agricultural journal. She organized and regularly attended conventions for women's rights. And she did all that while being a wife and the mother of eight children. Amy had heard her speak.

"She told the group about a Negro woman who is 6 feet tall and calls herself Sojourner Truth. Isn't that a wonderful name? She was born a slave but managed to escape. She became a Christian and promised to travel and stay in different places. That's what 'sojourn' means … and she would spread the truth. She advocates for abolition and women's rights…"

Ed gave Marty a private smile that seemed to say, "Well, this is our Amy …"

Ed and Marty may not have thought about women's rights before, but they recognized her enthusiasm for the cause as being what they might expect from Amy, who was feisty and serious about women's education.

∞∞∞

In September, after the harvest, Ed returned to Ripley.

Marty fell into a desultory mood. He knew Amy and his parents were also sad to see Ed leave. Marty had been happy to come home and see his family in Worthington, but now wished he had been able to go back to Ripley with Ed.

Bone was at his heels all the time. He seemed almost to sense Marty's thoughts and was afraid he'd leave again. Marty decided that if he should go back to Ripley, he would take Bone with him—even if it meant arguing with his father about it.

As the leaves turned the countryside orange and gold, he and Bone explored the area around the ravine and found the dugout where Ozem Gardner hid slaves. He didn't go inside but sat on a boulder thinking about the runaways his family had housed.

Thanksgiving 1858

The preparation of Thanksgiving dinner was a family affair. Amy and Marty were put in charge of the stuffing. They cubed the stale bread, chopped celery and onions, and put part of it inside the turkey. Mr. Spencer greased and trussed the turkey and slid it in the oven. Mrs. Spencer fixed mashed potatoes and gravy, green beans, and pumpkin pie with whipped cream.

Isaac was their dinner guest. After they'd eaten all they could hold of turkey and trimmings, they decided to give their stomachs a rest for a while before pumpkin pie. It was time for conversation. Isaac addressed Marty, "Tell me about Ripley, son."

So, he told him about sitting on the bench with Dan, watching the activity of the riverfront. He described John Parker strutting down the middle of the street and the Rankin house on the hill with its beacon. Isaac seemed captivated by the scenes Marty painted with his words.

Isaac wanted to know if he felt Ed was content, living with Uncle Seth and learning to make furniture. Marty wasn't entirely sure, but he said yes.

By the time the meal was over, it seemed that they were all in a lighter mood than they'd been in for quite a while.

Christmas 1858

On Christmas Day, Mr. and Mrs. Spencer made a momentous announcement. They had decided to sell the farm sometime within the next year or two. The news jolted Amy and Marty, but within a few hours, they found that they were less surprised than they'd initially felt. They realized there had been clues leading up to this decision during the past year. Ed's leaving meant that their parents recognized him as an adult who needed to make his own way. Even though they would no longer have his valuable help, they let him go. With their father's crippling arthritis came a slacking off farm duties and they'd sometimes sensed a malaise in him. Overall, he'd grown quieter, though he still enjoyed visiting with Isaac's group and was still passionate about abolitionist issues.

The main question in Amy and Marty's mind was where the family would live and how they would make a living. Their father said he hoped the money from the sale of the farm would be enough to buy them a small house in town and cover modest living expenses. Their mother wanted a place with a garden. She was a good seamstress and planned to open a custom clothing business to supplement their income.

But it would all be done gradually. Their announcement was meant to ease the children into it. They weren't in a hurry to sell the house. They would keep one cow for milk, and a horse and wagon. They would have at least one more garden season, preserving a lot of produce for future use. The farmland other than their sizable garden plot would be leased to someone who wanted to plant crops on it.

Amy's big concern was the question of tuition for Otterbein. She hoped to finish the present term and attend next year. Then, she would look for a teaching position. Her parents assured her that they intended to support her until she graduated.

1859

Dealing with Changes

In the New Year, Marty sometimes found himself feeling uneasy about all the changes. At other times, he felt curious and venturesome about what lay ahead.

To add to all the changes in his family, he was dealing with his own changes. He'd turned 13 and entered adolescence. He had grown three inches during the first six months of 1858, and Isaac started calling him "beanpole." He was now taller than his father and mother and Amy. He thought he might be taller than Ed and was eager to see him to find out. He was taller than the boy who had led the snowball assault on him last year after school. This year, he left him alone. His voice deepened and sometimes cracked; his body, though still slender, had filled out.

This was his last year of grammar school, but his parents insisted he would attend high school next year. He wasn't sure how he felt about that. He wondered what he would do in the adult world. Amy would be a teacher. Ed was learning how to build furniture. As yet, he had discovered no special skill or aptitude in himself. Marty remembered Ed's pride when he showed him how to make some sturdy dining room chairs. He'd said, "It's not that hard. I bet you could learn to do this, too." He knew he didn't have Ed's natural talent but wondered if he might end up helping Ed and Uncle Seth.

He had taken on more chores since Ed's departure, and he carried them out dutifully, although much of the time, he wished he could go back to Ripley. He sometimes felt guilty about this, like he was being disloyal to his parents.

Some afternoons, he went to Isaac's store and listened to his father and his friends shoot the breeze. Their main grievance was with the recent decision by the U.S. Supreme Court over Dred Scott, a slave living in a free state who sued for his freedom. The court ruled that Scott didn't have the right to sue because he was not a citizen. Slaves were not considered United States citizens. It also declared the Missouri Compromise, which stated that slavery could not be expanded in the free territories, was unconstitutional. Slavers were jubilant over the decision. Isaac and friends thought that slavers were gaining too much power in Congress and, with its decision, in the Supreme Court, too.

One thing Marty still wanted to know was what happened to the characters in *Uncle Tom's Cabin*. Amy was no longer inclined to read the book aloud. She said she was too busy with schoolwork, but she would give him the book to read himself. He said, "No, just tell me what happened."

"Okay, I'll give you a short summary of the plot. You'll be happy to know that Eliza and George Harris escaped to Canada with their son Harry, though there was a big fight with slave hunters on the way. For Uncle Tom, it started out well. He saved the life of a young woman named Eva St. Clare and became friends with her. Her father was grateful and bought Tom and treated him well. She was sickly and died. Her father was planning to free his slaves, but then he was killed when he tried to break up a fight. That was too bad for Uncle Tom because Eva's mother, who had always neglected her, was a hard woman. She sent Uncle Tom to a slave market. He was bought by a brutal man named Simon Legree, who got angry with Uncle Tom and beat him nearly to death. George Shelby, you remember him, came two days later wanting to buy Uncle Tom, but it was too late …

"I left out a lot. There are what is called subplots… But I told you about the main characters… And one more thing… you'll like this, Marty… When his father died, George Shelby released all of his family's slaves."

Marty had a lump in his throat but was determined not to be teary over Uncle Tom's fate. He remembered his father telling him once that he had to be tough, and, although he couldn't articulate exactly how, he knew that John Parker and Ripley had helped make him stronger.

A Different Room, Another Book

In early February, Marty asked his mother if he could move into Ed's room. He thought it was warmer at night than his own room. The real reasons were that somehow it made him feel closer to his brother and more grown up. His mother grumbled, saying she didn't see much difference in the temperature of the two rooms, and besides, she had already moved some of her things into the room where she planned to do her sewing. Marty pointed out that his room was nearer the top of the stairs and would be more convenient for her and said he would help her move her stuff if she would exchange rooms. Finally, she relented.

There was a small closet in the room that looked empty except for a pair of Ed's old boots. Marty tried the boots on and found them a little tight. He thought that not only he might be taller than Ed, he also had bigger feet. The boots weren't in very good condition—probably the reason Ed hadn't taken them with him. He shoved them back in the closet, thinking he would ask his parents what to do with them later. Closing the door, he caught sight of a book lying flat on the back of the small shelf at the top of the closet. Before his growth spurt, he might have missed it.

The title was *My Bondage and My Freedom*, written by Frederick Douglass.

He opened the book and saw that it was published in 1855. It was a February day with temperatures hovering around zero and the cold penetrated even the warmer room. Marty wrapped himself in a blanket, and propped in bed with a pillow, began to read. Though he thought the prose was wordy, he was immediately engrossed by the autobiography of an articulate former slave. He thought, this is a real story, told by a man who was a slave, not a made-up story like *Uncle Tom's Cabin*.

The first chapter about the author's early life was fine. Frederick Douglass lived with his grandparents in a small cabin. His grandmother was the most important person in his life. He loved her very much. He didn't think of himself as a slave and had a carefree life until around age seven when his grandmother took him to the Old Master's plantation twelve miles away. Thus, Douglass—though that was not his name then and he didn't even know his date of birth—walked many miles and began his sad life as a slave.

Marty wondered why no one in his family had mentioned this book. Amy must know about it. She seemed to know everything about literary things. He wondered if Ed had read it. After he read chapter three, he thought maybe he knew why no one in his family had mentioned it.

Douglass wrote about his mother who he rarely saw because she was a slave on another plantation several miles away, and she had to walk to see him. He knew that his father was of white heritage. Some people said it might be his own master.

But he didn't just talk about his own parentage, he talked of slavery in general:

> *... the fact remains, in all its glaring odiousness, that by the laws of slavery, children, in all cases, are reduced to the condition of their mothers. This arrangement admits of the greatest license to brutal slaveholders, and their profligate sons, brother, relations and friends, and gives to the pleasure of sin, the additional attraction of profit...*

Marty understood that he was talking about slave holders taking advantage of their female slaves and that force was involved. When children were born from these unions, they were often sold because "men do not love those who remind them of their sins…" Also, "such a child is a constant offense to the wife."

Maybe Douglass's frankness about slave masters having relationships with their slaves was the reason the book had been squirreled away on the0 top shelf of the closet.

News from Ripley

"A bit of bad news from Ripley," his mother told Marty, when he came home from school. Seeing the alarm in his eyes, she quickly added, "Don't worry. I didn't mean to scare you. It's a piece of bad luck, but not that bad. Uncle Seth has broken his left leg."

"Oh … that's not good. How can he do his work?"

"We'll wait 'til your father comes home and talk about it at dinner," she said, opening the oven to check on the gingerbread she was baking. "You need to go do your chores."

At dinner, Amy and Marty were eager to learn more about how the accident happened? How did their parents find out about it?

"We got a letter from Ed. It seems that Uncle Seth was on a ladder, trying to make a repair in a gutter, and he fell off," said their mother.

Mr. Spencer said, "Old fool … he shouldn't have been doing that. Should've had Ed do it or hired somebody."

"Now, Luke, he's not that old, only two years older than me… Shall we tell Marty…?"

"Go ahead."

"Well, Marty, Ed has the idea that you can return to Ripley and help him. He says that you learned some things while you were there, and he could teach you some more… He's got orders to fill, and Seth can still do some work, but he's limited…"

Marty tried to hide his elation at this news. "But what would you do without me to help?"

"Well, your mother and I will have to think about it … talk it over. Then, we can talk about it some more."

Later, Mrs. Spencer asked her husband, "Did you see Marty's eyes when I said Ed wanted him to come back to Ripley? They lit up like Christmas lights."

"Well, he seemed concerned about us—how we will manage without him, if he goes."

"Luke, I know he wants to go. We'll have to find other ways to manage."

And so, it was decided that Marty should go to Ripley. Mr. Spencer had learned of a Black freedman named Jonas who needed work and was recommended as a reliable person. The family found him personable and hired him on the same day he was interviewed.

Once again, Otto offered to make the trip to Ripley, this time with Bone included.

John Parker

In Ripley, Marty was kept busy helping Ed, but he sometimes managed to take a break, usually on Saturday afternoons to sit on the bench overlooking the Ohio River. One day when John Parker strode down the street, presumably on his way home from the riverfront, Marty rose and followed him. He thought he'd like to see Parker's home and his foundry that he'd heard was behind his home.

He was ambling along, trying not to be obvious, when he was distracted by a trilling sound. It was not like any bird song he'd ever heard.

Then, behind him came a question. "Are you followin' me, boy?"

Marty whipped around. "How—How…?"

"How did I get behind you? Strange, huh?" He grinned slyly. "So, again, are you followin' me?"

"I-I guess so," Marty stammered.

"Why?" Parker demanded.

"Well, I—I think you're a man my daddy told me about, and I just wondered…"

"Who is your daddy?"

"Luke—Luke Spencer."

"Never heard of him. Where does he live?"

"He—He doesn't live here. He—He lives in Worthington, Ohio."

"Never been there. Doesn't seem right to me."

"I—I think he learned about you at a meeting of … abolitionists."

"Abolitionist? That's a dangerous word around here. You know that?" He glared at Marty.

"I—I'm sorry. I didn't mean no harm." He turned around to start back towards his bench.

"Boy! Hey, boy! Turn around and talk to me!"

Marty became indignant. "My name is Martin—not boy!"

"Okay … Martin. Now tell me why you come to Ripley. I saw you sitting on the bench with old Dan—when was it? Last Spring? Then you disappeared. And here you are again watchin' me … followin' me."

"I—My brother is learnin' furniture makin' from our Uncle Seth, and I'm helpin' … what I can."

"Seth Porter? Yeah, I know him. Bought some furniture from him for my house. He banged up his leg. I've seen him hobbling' around on crutches."

Marty turned to leave again.

Parker called after him, "Martin, I close my foundry every day at 12 noon for lunch hour. You can come talk to me then if you want to, someday at the foundry …"

Marty nodded but kept walking.

∞∞∞

For a few days, Marty was angry at John Parker for the abrupt way he'd been treated. He wasn't sure he wanted to talk to him again. But then on Saturday, he volunteered to run an errand for Uncle Seth, telling Ed that he might be gone a while. He'd told him about Dan and how he liked to watch the activity on the river. He didn't tell him about John Parker. In fact, he wasn't sure he'd try to go to his foundry until he found himself walking that way. He found the door to the foundry locked and decided there was no one around, but as he turned to walk away, the door opened and John Parker called, "Come on in, boy."

"Martin—I'm Martin, remember?"

"Yep, sure do. I thought you probably wouldn't come."

Inside, it was hot and smelled of burnt metal.

John Parker reached under a counter and took out a bag with food in it. "You want part of a sandwich? It's pork, left over from last night's supper."

Marty nodded and said thanks. He felt shy and a bit scared. What would he talk to this man about?

But he didn't have to worry. John Parker started right in, telling him about his life. The belligerence he'd shown on their first meeting was gone.

"I was born a slave, but now I own my own business. Pretty good, huh?"

Marty nodded,

"Ya' know, my father was a white man, a southern aristocrat, owner of a plantation, but my ma was a slave. My father made no claim to me. When I was eight years old, he sold me. I was chained with a group of slaves and walked for miles and miles."

He stared at Marty as if taking his measure. "Does that shock you? My father being a white man and disowning me?"

"Nuh—No. We had a slave boy named Aron stay at our house once—him and his mama. My family told me he was a mulatto because he had white blood."

"Were they runaways?"

"Our family doesn't talk about runaways."

"What did your father tell you about me?"

"He said you have helped many slaves escape and that you are quite daring because you go into slave territory and lead them to freedom."

"Your father could be wrong … but, just say, if he were right … I agree with your family that it's best not to talk about runaway slaves. You know about John Rankin and his family who live in the house on the hill?"

Marty nodded yes.

"Did you know that his home was once under siege from slave hunters?"

"Yes."

"There are a lot of them still around, slave hunters, that is—some of them violent and looking to get rewards for capturing slaves and the people who help them—abolitionists. That's why it's best not to talk about runaways."

Marty nodded, "I know," he said.

∞∞∞

A week later, Marty found an excuse to get away and go visit John Parker again.

Parker told him more about his background.

"As far as slaves go, I probably had it better than most. I was owned by a doctor … although I tell you, I hate the word 'owned,' Anyway, I played with his sons. They taught me how to read and write. Most slaves don't know how to read and write, you know.

"But I always had the rebel in me. I had pride. I hated slavery and being a slave. I hated mistreatment, so I've been in a few scrapes in my life … had a few narrow escapes. Still, I had the chance to learn the foundry business and I was finally able to buy my freedom and start my own business."

And so it went. Marty came to Parker's Foundry at 12 noon, usually on Fridays, a couple of times a month.

And gradually secrets were divulged.

Parker told of inventing a plow and having a white employer take credit for it. Plows based on his invention were sold, but, of course, Parker received no money or recognition for it. Before he left the area where this happened, he beat the man up in a huge brawl.

He eventually got around to relating some of his escapades in rescuing slaves.

With bravado, Parker told Marty about sneaking into the house of slave owners at night while they were asleep and stealing a baby from the bottom of their bed. The baby's parents were slaves. Their owners kept the baby in their bedroom at night because they knew the slave parents would not try to escape without their baby. After he got the baby, he was able to lead the parents to freedom.

Another hair-raising tale took place in Ripley. Parker and two slaves were trapped by slave hunters. They managed to get into the workshop of a man named Collins, a coffin maker. The place was surrounded. Parker made the quivering slaves get inside the coffins. Then, he got in a coffin himself. The slave hunters came inside the workshop but never looked in the coffins.

One tale was humorous. He told of a woman who came dragging a bag nearly her own size, expecting to take it in the small boat crossing the river. She and a companion also had on skirts with large hoops that outsized the boat. They were even toting a frying pan which they thought to use to cook their meals on the way to Canada. They'd complained when he made them get rid of their hoops and their booty, but he told them it was either that, or he wouldn't help them. They complied.

Nailed to a tree, he'd once found a wanted poster for himself. Slave owners were offering a $1,000 bounty for his capture. "That's the reason I walk in the middle of the street. I don't want anyone jumping me out of an alley. And that's why I always carry a loaded pistol and a knife."

Each time Marty approached the foundry, he felt intimidated yet drawn. His visits with Parker filled him with feelings of intrigue and a touch of danger. He was becoming friends with a man who had survived by brawn and guile. He had injured, maybe killed people, and he himself had been injured and nearly killed. Some people would call Parker a criminal because of his help in freeing slaves. He had violated the Fugitive Slave Act some 400 times, according to his count.

Marty held onto these feelings in a special, secretive way. He still did not tell Ed or Uncle Seth about his visits with Parker.

And he did not tell Parker that family and friends called him by his nickname. When Parker addressed him, it was always by his given name, Martin. Marty, he thought, was childish. With Parker, he wanted to appear more grown-up.

And eventually Martin, not Marty, revealed his family's unlawful activities. He told Parker about Aron and how he and Aron encountered the two slave hunters in the ravine. He told him about Amy's basement school for Aron and his mama, Dora. And how Aron was dressed in Amy's clothes and taken away in the false bottom of a wagon. He told him about the slave hunters turning up at their door, demanding to search the house, and how his father stood up to them. And then, how the Marshal came and how his father let him search the house because they'd made sure all signs of the fugitives were removed.

Parker said, "Your father is a clever man."

Martin told about the hidden closet Ed had built in the attic and how slave hunters broke into their house when they were gone and how Joseph hid in the closet, and the slave hunters didn't find him. And he told him about Lena and how she was probably carrying Joseph's baby.

He told him about Ed and Amy and him taking produce to Delaware County in a wagon with a runaway hidden under the food and the two slave hunters following them.

He even told him about getting in a fight at school over the right language to use for Black people.

When Martin had told Parker all his secrets—his family's secrets—he made a big decision. He had an important question to ask him. One day he took a deep breath and asked, "Could … Would you let me help you … if you go across the river again to help people escape … would you let me help me in some way?"

"Boy! … Martin, you don't know what you're askin'. It's dangerous business. Even if the slavers don't capture me, your family would have my hide…"

∞∞∞

In mid-afternoon on a surprisingly mild day in August, Marty walked down the road going south from Ripley. There was a spring in his walk and a sense of excitement about his mission. He had a fishing pole on his shoulder and carried a can of worms. In his pocket, he had a strip of jerky for a snack. As he walked, he scanned the shore. About a mile outside of Ripley, he found what he was looking for—two logs lying together to form a 'T.' He started down the sandy slope toward the river, digging his heels in to keep from falling. His foot got caught in a root and he nearly fell but managed to land on his rear, keeping his can of worms upright. On the shore, he looked behind him and, again, found what he was looking for. It was a recess partially obscured by weeds and sand. A rocky overhang hid a hollowed-out area. In it was a small skiff, just like John Parker said there would be. It contained a rope for mooring and a spike on the shore had been hammered in the ground for that purpose.

This was part one of a three-part project John Parker had planned for Marty to help him. He was to locate the boat, get it in the water, moor it, get in it, bait his hook, and fish. Fishing was not the main objective, but if people traveling on the road should see him, they would see a boy engaged in an innocent activity and smile positively at him. And, well, if he did catch a fish that would be good. John Parker said he'd find a pole for him, but then Marty had found a fishing pole stashed in a corner of Uncle Seth's shed, and his uncle assented and smiled benevolently when he asked if he could use it. "Maybe we'll have catfish for dinner," he said.

One man on a horse stopped on the road and yelled, "Catch anything?"

Marty yelled back, "Not yet.

"Well, I wish you luck. It's a good day for fishin'."

A few nights later, Marty sneaked out and walked down the same road. He had his fishing pole and a bucket. The bucket held a small candle lantern, one of John Parker's own creations. The reason the lantern was in the bucket was he didn't want to call attention to himself. But the candle was lit and gave enough light for Marty to find his way. His bucket also held a small can of worms, though like the first trip, fishing was for appearances only. It was not the objective. Marty found the logs that formed a "T" and was able to traverse the slope more skillfully than he did the first time, even though it was dark. He found the skiff and wrested it from its hiding place. He moored it and climbed in it to fish, but his eyes were on the Kentucky shore, scanning and waiting. Beneath the quarter moon, the night was peaceful with an almost indiscernible gurgle from the river. Now and then, a bullfrog croaked and a dog barked in the far distance. Marty fought off drowsiness.

After a few minutes, he saw what he'd been looking for, the flash of a lantern, then another flash—five flashes about a minute apart and a few feet between each. He wanted to hold up his lantern to let John Parker know he'd seen his signals. But that wasn't the plan. Solitary flashes on the Kentucky shore could mean a person engaged in an insignificant activity, but an exchange of lights might make someone suspicious— someone unfriendly to the rescue of runaway slaves.

The next day, Marty told Parker that he had seen the five flashes, and what had been a dress rehearsal was set in motion for the real thing. Two nights later, Marty slipped out of Uncle Seth's house at night. Again, he had a bucket with candle lamp and his fishing pole. He found the canoe and something that hadn't been there before, a box that contained a blanket and some food. He sat in the canoe, fishing while watching for the flashes across the river. As soon as the flashes ended, he dragged the canoe out of the water and placed the blanket and food in it. Then, he started out in haste. When he reached the road, he broke into a run. Breathlessly, he climbed the hill to the Rankin house and knocked on the door, which was opened quickly by one of John Rankin's tall sons.

"I have a message from John Parker," Marty said. "A package will soon be delivered."

The man smiled and thanked him. "We'll take care of it," he said.

Meanwhile, Parker rowed across the river with a scared, shivering Negro man curled up in his skiff. He reached Marty's fishing spot and had the runaway get in the other skiff. He wrapped the blanket around his shoulders and showed him the food—an apple and a ham sandwich—that Marty had left. Then, he told him he had to stay in the skiff in the dark hiding place. "Don't come out until I come and get you! Understand?"

Parker dragged the other skiff several yards away and hid it among some weeds. He then went up to the road and scouted the area. Several minutes later, he came back to the hiding place and led the runaway through a circuitous route to the back of the Rankin house.

Thus, Marty had participated in his first rescue without having direct contact with the fugitive.

The next day when Marty went to the foundry, Parker said, "Good job, Martin. Are you ready to do it again next week?"

The same thing was repeated the following week, except this time Marty went to the home of a family named Collins. This time a kind-looking woman answered the door. She said, "Thank you, son. My husband will see to it."

The third episode took place a month or so later. This time, as Marty went some distance down the road, he had the feeling he was being followed. Quickly, he stepped behind a tree and, in the moonlight, saw the unmistakable silhouette of his brother.

Ed stopped walking and called, "Marty!" He resumed walking slowly but then stopped and called again. "Marty … Marty, are you hiding from me?"

Then, he called again, louder. Afraid that someone would hear his brother and that his plans would be aborted, Marty stepped out of the shadows. "Sh-h. You shouldn't be followin' me."

"And why not? You snuck out of the house at night, and you're pretty far from home… I don't think this is the first time, is it? I'm supposed to be the guardian of you when you're in Ripley."

"I didn't hear Daddy appoint you as my guardian." Marty was surprised at the defiance in his voice. This was Ed, the brother he loved and looked up to.

"You know what I mean, Marty. I'm supposed to look after you when our parents are not around."

"I'm not a baby!"

"No, but … I'm to look after you … Sneaking out at night? I don't think Uncle Seth would like that either."

"Look, I gotta go. I'm helping someone… It's a good thing."

"Who are you helping?"

"John Parker."

"The John Parker? You're not crossing the river with him, are you?" Ed tried to whisper, but the tone of his voice was shrill.

"Sh-h! No, I just have to deliver a message when I see his flares, that's all. I never even see the slaves… I gotta go."

"All right, Marty, I'll go home and wait for you, and then we can talk. But please, please be careful."

"Don't worry. I've done it before."

Marty took off half running, half walking, afraid he would be late for Parker's signals, but all was okay. He waited about five minutes and saw the first flash. He went through what was now a routine—take the skiff out of the water, put the food and blanket in it, and shove it under the overhang. Then, he hurried to take his message to a house where a family named Evans lived.

Marty could see the relief on Ed's face when he walked through the door. He wanted to know the whole story about his relationship and his illicit activities with John Parker.

"Look, Marty, I can see you've been doing good things with Parker, but can you understand that I'm afraid that something could go wrong and you could get hurt?"

"Um, yeah … I guess."

"I don't want you to do it anymore, okay?"

Marty hung his head and nodded.

"I think I should meet Parker and talk to him."

"I-I asked … to help him. Don't … don't blame him."

Privately, Ed regarded his brother with concern, yes, but also with some amusement and admiration. He knew that John Parker was a man whose reputation many found daunting. There was a fierceness about him, and people gave him a wide berth. It had taken some pluck for Marty to become acquainted, let alone to develop a friendship with him.

As he lay in bed that night thinking about the situation, Ed came to appreciate Parker's ingenuity. He had come up with a scheme that was low risk for Marty but also made him feel he was helping. Intuitively, he realized that a bond had developed between the man and his brother.

∞∞∞

"Hi Marty, it's been a few days since I've seen you. You didn't come in the day after our last adventure."

Marty knew as soon as he heard Parker use the familiar form of his name that Ed had been talking to him.

"Everything went okay?"

"Yeah … except …"

"Except your brother found out what you were doing?"

"Yeah."

"He came to see me. He doesn't want you to help me anymore."

"Yeah … I know." Marty scowled.

"Well, he seems like a good guy, just concerned for your safety."

For a few minutes, they sat in comfortable silence.

"You once mentioned to me that your father told you about Levi Coffin."

"Yeah, he said he was known as President of the Underground Railroad."

"Well, I think that title should belong to me." Parker smiled and Marty could tell he was joking, kind of.

"Would you like to meet him?"

Marty brightened. "Levi Coffin, you mean?"

"Yes."

"He's lives in Cincinnati, don't he?"

"Yes, in the Cincinnati area. If you'd like to meet him, maybe I could arrange it."

"Sure, I'd like that a lot."

Luke & Virginia Spencer in Ripley

Marty was excited. His mother and father and Amy were planning to spend some time in Ripley. He couldn't wait to show them all the skills he had learned in furniture making. He wanted to show his father the Rankin house on the hill at night and say, "Look, it's just like you said. They have a lantern lit so runaways can find the way to their house."

He wanted to show them his treasured view of the Ohio River where he sat on the bench with Dan and where he had, one day, dared to rise and follow John Parker—an action that changed his life in new and exciting ways. He was hesitant to introduce them to Parker, afraid that Ed had told them about his nighttime adventures. He felt sure they would disapprove of him engaging in what they might consider dangerous activities. Besides, his friendship with Parker was a part of his life that made him feel grown-up and able to make his own decisions. A part of him was secretive about it. Parker had promised him they would visit Levi Coffin sometime soon. If that happened and the visit went well, he knew he would tell his parents about it at some later date. It would be a coup of sorts.

Not long after they arrived, a rider galloped into the center of town and jumped off his horse, yelling that he had news people needed to hear. Soon, a group surrounded the man, who appeared to be in his early twenties. He had a story to tell but was so excited he was almost incoherent. Dan was one of the men in the crowd. He said, "Calm down, son, and tell us what happened!"

"A man—John Brown is his name—he led a group of men … they attacked a federal armory in Harper's Ferry … in Virginia."

"Who is John Brown?" someone in the crowd asked.

Luke Spencer, who had been out strolling, getting acquainted with the town, joined the crowd. He spoke up. "I know who he is. He's a radical abolitionist who led some raids in Kansas."

"The men in the Harper's Ferry raid—were any of them Negroes? I 'm askin' because I wonder if Brown led Negroes in a rebellion," Luke Spencer said.

"I'm not sure … I think there might have been."

In the following days, details were filtered in from other sources.

John Brown had rented a farmhouse just outside of Harper's Ferry under a false name. He had amassed a group of 21 men to lead an insurrection. His goal was to capture weapons from the arsenal and rouse slaves to carry out a rebellion across the South.

The group attacked and took over the arsenal. They cut the telegraph wires but made a mistake when they let a train pass through. The conductor wired the home office, and the home office notified President Buchanan and the Virginia governor. Meanwhile, local people with weapons surrounded the arsenal and took command of a bridge so there was no escape route. Then, a federal force came in and quelled the insurrection.

Brown's men killed four people and wounded several more. Federal forces killed ten of Brown's men, including two of his sons. Brown was wounded. He was captured and tried for murder and treason. In December came news of his execution. Two Negro men from Oberlin, Ohio, involved in the attack were also hanged.

Although people didn't support such violence to end slavery, many Ohioans had sympathy for John Brown and his men. In some towns on the day of execution, church bells rang, flags flew at half mast, businesses closed, and crowds gathered in support. Amy came up with the right term for Brown. He would be considered a martyr. A newspaper reported that 3,000 people attended the funeral held for the two Oberlin men.

In the South, it was a different story. People feared other violent uprisings against slavery.

Mr. Spencer who had always maintained that there would be skirmishes, but not broader conflict, began to voice misgivings. He'd heard rumblings about southern states seceding from the union and feared the Harpers Ferry incident would push the South toward stronger action.

Thanksgiving 1859

Mrs. Spencer wanted to cook a turkey for the holiday meal. Seth said he had a nice, cured ham, but she insisted on turkey. So, he contacted a man who had a farm and brought home a bird to please his sister. They had a wonderful dinner with turkey and dressing, yams, green beans, and a choice of pumpkin and apple pie. Ed and Marty realized how much they had missed their mother's cooking.

The day was gray and blustery and gave rise to solemn thoughts and conversation about the tragedy of Harper's Ferry and its possible effect on worsening relations between North and South.

Mr. Spencer commented that he had heard that John Brown had met with the former slave and orator Frederick Douglass and tried to persuade him to conspire with his group to lead an extended insurrection in the South. Douglass had declined.

Marty who had been intent on enjoying his dinner startled his family by saying, "He didn't do that because he's too smart."

Mr. Spencer asked, "And how do you know about Frederick Douglass?"

"I-I read his book. I found it in the closet in my room … in Worthington. He's a mulatto, like Aron…, you know. He wrote about it in his book."

Then, as though he couldn't drop the subject after being brave enough to have brought it up, he plunged on. "John Parker … here, in Ripley, he's also a mulatto."

Amy and Ed exchanged amused glances. Mrs. Spencer blushed and looked down at her plate. Mr. Spencer said, "Well that sometimes happened." Seth cleared his throat and said, "I know Parker. He bought some furniture from me several years ago. He runs a foundry, and he's a good businessman."

Mr. Spencer asked Marty, "And how did you meet Parker?"

"Well, I-I met him once in town," he said, being purposely vague, but then added, "And he- he knows Levi Coffin, and he said he might take me to meet him sometime … in Cincinnati."

Mrs. Spencer said, "My goodness!"

Though rarely surprised, Mr. Spencer said, "Now, that would be something!"

Seth and Mr. Spencer talked about national politics. Listening to them, Marty realized how much he missed hearing those conversations in Isaac's store. One topic of conversation was the debates between Abraham Lincoln and Stephen Douglas when they vied for the office of Senator from Illinois.

"What do you think of this fella Lincoln. Six foot-four, they say. It was the tall and short of it—I heard Douglas is only 5 foot 4. The 'Little Giant,' they call Douglas. He strutted around all theatrical, while Lincoln just stood still and made his points. Lincoln looks like a scarecrow to me, but he sure could talk," said Seth.

"Yes, I was impressed by him. Douglas defeated him, but I don't think we've heard the last of Abraham Lincoln."

"He's against slavery, isn't he?"

"Yep, it seems so. He thinks it's a moral issue. I don't think Douglas cares. He believes in what is called 'popular sovereignty,' which lets the people vote on whether there should be slavery in a state, particularly in Kansas. Under the Missouri Compromise passed so long ago in 1820, Missouri was granted statehood, but the rest of the Louisiana Purchase would be free. Under that law, Kansas should be a free state.

"There's a lot of violence going on in Kansas between slavers and non-slavers. Otto, the peddler, who brought Marty to Ripley, has spent time in Kansas and seen what goes on there."

"Well, I hear tell there's some of that that goes on right here in Ripley, too." That was an understatement because Seth was aware of the abolitionist activity around him, but he stayed out of it. Although he thought slavery was wrong, he didn't want to engage in activity that might harm his business. No one in the Spencer family had told him about how they helped fugitives in Worthington. And, of course, Ed didn't tell him about Marty's activities with John Parker. If his uncle suspected anything, he didn't say so.

"It's interesting that Lincoln quoted the proverb, 'A house divided against itself cannot stand.' He believes the union will not be dissolved, but he said it 'cannot endure … half slave and half free.' Now, how that's settled, I'd like to know…," said Spence.

At the end of the meal, Mr. and Mrs. Spencer made a surprise announcement. They had been talking to Seth about the possibility of moving to the Ripley area. Amy would soon graduate and hoped to get a teaching job in Cincinnati, which was only about 50 miles from Ripley. The family could be close together. Meanwhile, Seth, along with Ed and Marty would scout the area for a suitable home for them.

1860

Building a Cabin

On Saturdays in the early spring, Marty and Ed accompanied Uncle Seth to search for possible houses for Luke and Virginia Spencer. They did this for three weeks in a row and didn't find anything suitable. One day, he asked Ed and Marty what they would think of building a house on his property. He owned some ten acres of woodland behind his house and shop.

"But it's all woods …," said Ed.

"Yes, it would involve clearing some trees. There is one place where there is a small clearing. Clearing around that would be easier… I know of some men who might do that for us. I think we could do some of the building ourselves and call in some builders for things we can't do."

Ed and Marty agreed and, as the days passed, they became excited to start the project.

Ed suggested they build a log cabin. It could have a large kitchen/sitting area combined, a small bedroom on the ground floor, and a divided loft that would sleep two people. They wrote to Mr. and Mrs. Spencer, asking for their approval.

Virginia Spencer said she'd always wanted to live in a log cabin, and so, in April 1860, the project began.

∞∞∞

Soon after the land was cleared, they received word from the Spencers. They were eager to start their new life in Ripley, and they wanted to do what they could to help with building their new home. Virginia Spencer was sure that she and Amy could provide a needed feminine touch. She said she could take over the cooking and free Seth to do other things. And so, they came in a carriage which they said was "too fancy" for them, but which Isaac had helped them find secondhand at a good price. Luke and Virginia would make do with a room in the back of the furniture shop until the cabin was built. It was a storage room used for odds and ends, but everything was cleared out and a bed and dresser installed, as well as a small makeshift closet in one corner, it was a suitable temporary bedroom. Seth's house was spacious enough that Marty and Ed each had a small bedroom, but they said they would now share one of the rooms in the new house and free the other up for Amy.

Virginia took command of the kitchen, but Seth, as a long-time bachelor, had developed his culinary skills and often joined her to fix one of his specialties. Their parents were middle-aged when they were born, and they learned to fend for themselves and cooperate to help their parents. After many years of separation, they fell into a companionable relationship that had been formed in childhood.

It was satisfying to watch the cabin grow from a skeleton into a habitable structure. The goal was to have it finished by the time the October chill fell on Ripley.

Levi Coffin

One Saturday, Parker and Marty traveled to Levi Coffin's home in a one-horse buggy.

Levi Coffin was a man with a severe demeanor, yet there was no impression of meanness. There was a firmness and assuredness about him, and after he talked for a while, Marty detected humor in his eyes.

He had a proclivity to teach and tell stories. Marty, a teenage boy who had participated in abolition activities, was a rapt listener.

He told Marty he was born in 1798 in North Carolina, a slave state, but his family did not believe in slavery. He said he had become an abolitionist at the young age of seven when he was standing near the roadside where his father was chopping wood. A coffle of slaves passed by, driven by a man on horseback with a whip. His father asked one of the slaves why they were bound. The man said that the owner wanted to prevent them from escaping and returning to their wives and children. This made Levi sad. By the time he was in his teens, he was helping his family hide runaways on their farm. As a young man in his early twenties, he and his cousin, Vestal Coffin, started a school to teach slaves to read the Bible, but slave owners got wind of it and shut it down.

Many members of his religion, the Society of Friends, called Quakers, began to leave North Carolina because they were persecuted if they were suspected of harboring slaves. In 1822, Levi also left with a group of people going to Indiana, a free state.

Levi's wife, Catherine, came in and offered hot chocolate and cookies. She looked a lot like Levi, stern but kind. Marty thought they looked enough alike to be brother and sister. John Parker had told Marty that she was an active and daring partner with her husband in hiding slaves. She got up in the middle of the night and made meals for fugitives. Sometimes they arrived cold and rain-soaked, and she saw that they had warm, dry clothing. She had organized a sewing society to make clothes especially for runaways and kept a collection of garments ready as needed.

Levi continued with a story of traveling with his brother-in-law and his family to Indiana. He made the story interesting and lively by describing a group of ruffians who approached the party and wanted to search their wagons. They said they had lost a dog and suspected that it was being hidden in a wagon. They were probably slave hunters looking for a runaway. Some Kentuckians who had joined the party of travelers refused to let the men search their wagon, even though they harbored no slaves. One man dared to hold off the ruffians with a whip, and finally, they left.

Another story was about how Levi went into the woods by himself in search of game and encountered a large bear. He shot the bear but didn't kill him. The bear was enraged with the injury and charged. Levi turned and ran, calling the dogs. The dogs attacked the bear but suffered scratches and hard blows. He and the other men tried to pursue the bear, but the injured dogs were tired and leery, and they had to give up.

"In our home in Indiana, we had a garret in our bedroom—a small room where we could hide runaways. We could slide our beds over so the bed boards would hide the door to the garret. We also had a wagon that had a good place for hiding people. We would put large, filled grain sacks around them. It worked very well."

Then, Levi turned more pedantic.

"Do you know the words 'manumission' and 'colonization'?" he addressed Marty.

Marty shook his head no.

"Well, they are long words but important. Manumission is the freeing of slaves by a master. But what happens to the slaves after they are freed is a matter of controversy. There are people who favor colonization, which means they should be sent to Africa. Other people believe they should be allowed to stay in the United States and prosper as they will. People in favor of them staying suspect that the other side, usually slave owners, want to get rid of free Blacks, so they don't stir up trouble. Sometimes, the former owners argue that when Blacks are free, they are no longer of value to the country. There is an American Manumission Society, and local manumission organizations. I belonged to one once. There was so much controversy that the people who favored colonization and those who did not split up. I belonged to the group that didn't favor colonization. These are things a young abolitionist such as you should know about."

It was nearing 4 p.m., and John Parker said they should be on the road before it turned dark.

Before they left, Marty, who had mostly listened, got brave enough to ask, "D-do you know that some people say you're the President of the Underground Railroad?"

"Well, I have met some runaways in my time … but maybe that title should belong to John here." With a twinkle in his eye, he nodded at John Parker.

Jonah

Walking a familiar route, Marty strode toward the riverbank spot where he'd watched for John Parker's lantern signals on those nights when he'd helped him. Bone followed him, seeming happy to be included in the outing. It was Sunday afternoon, and the furniture shop was closed. His family were all into their own private pursuits. His mother was sewing, his father was reading a paper, Uncle Seth was taking a hike through the woods, and Ed had gone courting. Yes, Ed had found a girl, and now he walked around with a dreamy look in his eyes. Her name was Dorothea. She was petite with ebony hair and ivory skin.

Marty was restless. He wanted to go see John Parker, but, of course, his foundry was closed on Sunday, and he didn't feel right going to his home. So, finally, he decided to get his fishing pole and some bait and set out for the river to what he'd come to think of as the "secret place." He scrambled down the embankment and looked under the overhang. He tried to pull the skiff out. He tugged on it, but it was heavy.

He jumped back, startled when a man sat up. The man had been sleeping, but his grogginess quickly changed to fright. "Don't tell on me! Please, mister, don't tell!"

Bone growled at the man. Marty shushed him.

Marty judged the man to be just a few years older than himself. He appeared to be about 5 foot, 6 inches tall, with a slender build and long, tangled dark hair and light coppery skin.

Marty said no, he wouldn't tell. He got the man to calm down and tell him that he had escaped from a plantation in Kentucky. He knew of John Parker and wanted to find him. He'd come across the river farther south and had looked for this hiding place that he'd learned about from other slaves. He pleaded for Marty to help him.

Marty said he'd try, but he'd have to get someone else to help.

The man looked alarmed. "You gonna tell somebody else where I is?"

"Don't worry. It will be a friend to runaways. Maybe John Parker if I can find him. Promise me you'll just stay here, and I'll try to come back tonight. My name is Marty. What's your name?"

"Jonah."

He gave Jonah a biscuit he'd brought along for a snack and again urged him to wait.

Marty climbed the embankment and then stopped and took a deep breath. He wasn't sure what he was going to do, but he was determined to help. He hightailed it for town. He started walking toward John Parker's house on Front Street but stopped when he saw two men loitering on the side of the street. They were hard-looking, bearded men who carried pistols in holsters. They reminded him of the men he and Aron encountered in the ravine several years ago. Ruthless men, men on the move, probably in search of runaway slaves that would bring them handsome rewards. They had horses and were rubbing them down. Marty wondered if that was a pretense to watch Parker's house. It was late afternoon, still daylight. He wondered if they would be somewhere near Parker's home in the evening.

What to do now? He felt timid about going to the Rankin's house but summoned his nerve, climbed the hill, and knocked on their door. This time, Reverend Rankin answered the door. Marty had never seen him, even from a distance, but he knew the man had to be the Reverend Rankin. He was tall, sixtyish, handsome, and dignified. He had white hair combed back from the sides and thinning on the top. Caring eyes gazed at Marty over a straight, elegant nose—a nose that lent special authority. Marty thought he might look like God, if ever God took a human form.

Reverend Rankin said, "You've been here before, haven't you, son, helping Parker?"

"Y-yes."

Marty was tongue-tied, but the Reverend waited patiently until he found the nerve to explain the situation.

"Have you tried to find Parker?"

Marty nodded. "I was going to his house, but I saw some men I thought might be slave hunters… I turned around…"

"Do you have anyone else to help you?"

"W-well, maybe my pa and my brother…" Marty explained about Uncle Seth's business and how his family had come to move to Ripley.

"We know Seth. Good man, but he doesn't get involved in the abolition business … Has your other family ever hidden runaways before?"

"Y-yes, but not here. We hid some people when we lived in Worthington."

"So, you know something about it. Do you think you could keep the man overnight and bring him to our barn in a wagon tomorrow, like you're delivering some furniture? If you brought him tonight … on a Sunday … a delivery might look suspicious.

"You're right. The men you saw were probably slave hunters. This area is crawling with them. They're watching us with eagle eyes because there's thought to be several runaways in the area with big prices on their heads. We're sure to be followed if we try to pick the man up tonight because we'd have to use a lantern. If you can keep him hidden tonight and bring him tomorrow, we'll be watching for him."

Marty left, feeling dismayed. It was getting late in the afternoon. His family would wonder where he was. Soon, the sun would set. He would have to explain everything to Ed and maybe his father to get them to help… But he knew his father had said he had no intention to get involved in hiding slaves in Ripley. He said Seth wouldn't like it.

Marty went home and ate dinner with his family. He was quiet, still pondering what to do about Jonah.

"What'd you do this afternoon?" his father asked him.

"Oh, I fished … didn't catch anything though…"

After dinner, he managed to get Ed alone and tell him about Jonah.

"Marty, Mr. Rankin was right. If we go out tonight with a wagon or the buggy, slave hunters might see our lantern and follow us. Let me think … maybe we could pick him up early in the morning…"

"But I told him I'd be back tonight."

"Can't be helped. What does Jonah look like? How big is he?"

"He's a small man, shorter than me."

"That's good. I'm thinking I could get Pa's buggy ready and maybe we could pick him up early in the morning, soon as it gets light out. We'll cover him up or maybe have him curl up in a gunnysack…"

The buggy was the vehicle their parents had used to make the trip to Ripley. Mr. Spencer had searched far and wide to find a buggy that would be suitable and affordable. This one had a folding top with protective flaps over two passenger seats. They hadn't brought much with them, just a few clothes, some of Mrs. Spencer's sewing items, food for snacks, and a jug of water. The buggy was full, but they managed.

"Are you gonna tell Pa?"

"I don't like to hide things from him … but I don't want to involve him in it either. You know, he said no more hiding runaways because Uncle Seth wouldn't like it. I'll make up a story about needing to go to see Dorothea before the shop opens…"

Marty went to bed at 8 o'clock but two hours later, woke with a start. He'd had a nightmare that slave hunters were approaching the secret place about to capture Jonah. He got dressed and found the candle lantern and the bucket he carried it in. He went to the pantry and found some biscuits and jerky. Then, he grabbed the fishing pole, just in case he met someone and needed an excuse for being out in the night. He started out the door but then came back and found a light blanket to throw around his shoulders.

At first, he thought that Jonah was gone. The canoe was in the water but had been moored. Then, he saw Jonah sitting a few feet away on the riverbank.

He jumped up when he saw Marty.

"Don't be scared. It's me, Marty. Here, I brought you some food."

"Oh mister, I so hungry I was eating grass … thought I might catch a minnow and eat it. I jus' couldn't stay in that cave no more."

"Look, you got to hold on a few more hours. When it starts to get light, my brother will come with a buggy. We'll take you to our house. I'm gonna put the canoe back in the … cave, and it's best you get in it." He hadn't thought of the overhang as a cave before but that seemed an apt enough name for it.

"I brought a blanket. Maybe it'll help if you cover your face with it."

Back home, Ed woke up when he heard Marty come in. He was sure he knew where he'd been.

About 5 a.m., Ed went out and hitched the horse to the buggy. They took off, hoping that any slave hunters would still be sleeping. Ed stopped the buggy near the embankment of the secret place. Marty found Jonah waiting, the blanket around his shoulders. They had him curl up in one of the buggy's seats, and Ed covered him with something he'd made. It was a box, except that it lacked a back and a bottom—a simple construction he'd put together after Marty had gone to bed.

They passed one lone rider on horseback. Ed tipped his hat and said, "Mornin'. Looks like it'll be a nice day." The man looked a little surprised at Ed's cheerfulness but nodded and rode on.

They hid Jonah in a woodshed behind the cabin.

Later in the morning, Ed asked Uncle Seth about picking up a load of lumber that had been planned for a week or so. He agreed that Seth could take the wagon and pick it up in the afternoon. Marty was to go with him.

Just before they left, Ed brought out a bench, one of several that had been in the showroom but with changes. Ed had converted it so that there was an enclosed storage bin under the seat. That space was where Jonah was to be hidden. It would be a tight fit, but it would work. Ed also put a small lamp table on the wagon.

"We'll just act like we're delivering furniture to the Rankins," he said. And that's what they did. Before they picked up the lumber, they went to the Rankin home. Marty was in awe of Ed's talents and the calm way he handled things.

That night at dinner, Mr. Spencer held his sons in a stern gaze that made them feel like he could see right through them. Then, he commented, "I think there are things going on around here that I haven't been told about."

Virginia Spencer said, "Oh, for heaven's sake, Luke, what do you mean by that?"

No more was said, but Ed and Marty knew that their father knew.

Thanksgiving 1860

All were thankful that the cabin was nearly completed. It was habitable but needed some finishing touches that could be done as time and weather permitted.

"Lincoln is a good man. Too good for the South. They're afraid he will take away their slaves," Mr. Spencer said, between mouthfuls of pumpkin pie.

"He ran on a platform that included prohibition of slavery in new states and territories, but he said he won't interfere with the internal affairs of the Southern states," Seth proffered.

"Still, some are talking secession… I don't think they trust Lincoln. And they don't want to hear anything about how the practice of slavery is a moral wrong. He kind of said that in his debates with Douglas. And he did quote the scripture that says, 'a house divided against itself cannot stand.'"

Tired of serious political talk, Amy said, "Let's talk about Mother's new business. She made Sunday dresses for Mrs. Bell's twins, and Mrs. Bell was so pleased, she is telling all her friends."

"They were just simple frocks—same pattern, in different colors."

"You're too modest, Mother. They were really nice."

"We're proud of you, Ginny," said her husband.

"Thank you, Luke. Thank you, Amy. And I am so thankful this year for our cozy new home and my wonderful family. It's nice to be close to Seth again. I miss Ed at the table, but I understand that Dorothea wanted him to have Thanksgiving fare with her family."

No one said so, but they all thought that Ed and Dorothea might be getting married soon.

Amy directed the conversation to Marty, "Marty, tell us again about your visit with Levi Coffin. That's so fascinating. I wish I could meet him."

So, even though they knew they had heard some of it before, they listened in rapt attention as Marty talked about his visit. And he added some things.

"John Parker told me that Levi Coffin has made trips to Canada to visit the former slaves he'd helped to free. He wanted to make sure they were doing okay. He also helped establish an orphanage for Negro children in Cincinnati. He's a really good man."

∞∞∞

The Thanksgiving dinner conversation between Luke Spencer and Seth Porter presaged the first disturbing event that threatened the soundness of the Union. On December 20, 1860, South Carolina became the first state to secede.

PART II: CIVIL WAR (1861-1865)

1861

A Nation Divided

In January, South Carolina was followed by Mississippi, Florida, Alabama, Georgia, Louisiana, and, in February, Texas.

"They're falling like dominos," said Seth.

The seceding states became the Confederate States of America.

"I'm afraid the Union is broken," said Luke Spencer. "I always thought they would come up with a solution—that it wouldn't actually happen. I'd like to think the South will still come to its senses…"

Then, on April 12, a neighbor brought the news that the South Carolina militia had seized all Federal property around the city of Charleston and had fired on Fort Sumter which was manned by Union troops.

And later, Union troops garrisoned in Fort Sumter surrendered.

Then, most alarming of all, President Lincoln called for 75,000 volunteers to quell the rebellion. In response four more states—Virginia, Tennessee, Arkansas, and North Carolina—joined the Confederacy.

Was the nation at war? It was difficult for the Spencer household—and the citizens of Ripley—to comprehend.

There was an air of incredulity about the impending war. It was unthinkable that citizens of the Union would be fighting each other in a wholesale conflict. It seemed like something that was happening in a foreign land. Brothers could be fighting brothers, some people said.

The first battle after Fort Sumter on July 21, 1861, made it all too real. It took place at Bull Run Creek in Manassas, Virginia, some 25 miles from the Capitol. The fighting was fierce and bloody. There were an estimated 4,700 casualties.

Although the Confederates were declared the victors, it was said that neither side was really trained and prepared for the conflict. From a distance, people brought lunches and viewed it with field glasses.

Virginia Spencer shook her head in disbelief. "They're treating it as sport, like watching a horse race."

Luke Spencer commented, "Maybe now, with so many deaths, leaders will come to their senses."

Throughout 1861, life for the Spencers and Seth Porter went on as usual.

Though they heard news of skirmishes in other states, the war seemed remote, not quite real.

1862

A Nation at War

If there was any hope that leaders might "come to their senses," it vanished with the two-day battle of Shiloh in Tennessee in April 1862. Shiloh was the name of a church which came to be used as a field hospital. General Ulysses S. Grant, an Ohioan, led the Union troops. His army was victorious but at great cost. The dead and wounded were reported as 23,000. Reportedly, it was the bloodiest battle in American history.

"Shiloh is a Biblical place. It means a 'place of peace,'" Amy told her family, after doing some research. "It was a sanctuary for the Israelites and the site of a tabernacle where the Ark of the Covenant was kept until its capture by the Philistines. The Ark of the Covenant was a chest that contained tablets with ten commandments etched on them—maybe we remember that from Sunday School… But the Biblical Shiloh was destroyed, too—maybe by the Philistines."

"Shiloh in Tennessee--a place of peace? 23,000 casualties! A place of shame and destruction, I'd say!" said her mother.

Virginia Spencer was normally self-possessed and sparing in words. Her strength expressed itself in a pervasive calmness and common-sense observations. In contrast, her husband Luke was voluble, a man who enjoyed explication and instruction. On those evenings in Worthington, when he talked at length, schooling their children on slavery and abolitionism, she had sat quietly with her knitting. While he talked and the children listened and asked questions, she created scarves, sweaters, and shawls for family and friends. There was a tacit recognition in the family that their father gained strength from her quiet presence.

But the escalating civil war unearthed an emotionalism in her. At day's end, in the privacy of their bedroom, her anxieties reached their apex and spilled out onto her husband like pouring a bucket of cold water on his head. It was like she had barely managed to hold them in all day. What a waste, this war! What was it about? All those fine young men being slaughtered, and for what? How would it touch their family? She couldn't bear the thought of Ed and Marty going off to kill others … and, unthinkably, perhaps to be killed. That an Ohioan, General Grant, had led the Battle of Shiloh, brought the war closer. Luke Spencer could only murmur, "I know, Ginny, I know. I worry, too."

In September 1862, Confederate forces captured Lexington, Kentucky. Commander Kirby Smith dispatched troops to capture Covington, Kentucky and Cincinnati, Ohio. The Union General Lewis Wallace was ordered to lead troops to defend the cities. He called for a volunteer militia. They were called to labor, not to battle. It meant preparing trenches and other duties to prepare for an attack. Nearly 16,000 men answered the call.

Ed Spencer was one of them. His mother was afraid that her fears had been realized.

But it turned out that Confederate forces withdrew from Kentucky, and Cincinnati was no longer in danger.

Ed came home in a heightened mood. He liked being part of a group that was defending Ohio. He felt certain that had Cincinnati been invaded, the attack would not have been successful because of the defenses they had set up. He told his family that he had slept in a church that became a barracks for the volunteers. The volunteers came to be known as the "squirrel hunters," because they had no previous military experience, and their weapons were more suited to small game hunting than combat. General Wallace became known as the "Savior of Cincinnati."

"You will never guess who I met in Cincinnati," Ed told the family during his first supper at home. "It was someone we knew in Worthington."

No one ventured a guess.

"Well, tell us, tell us. Don't keep us in suspense!" Amy demanded.

"Aron, the boy we hid in our attic."

"Aron … why was he in Cincinnati? He is supposed to be in Canada," said Mr. Spencer.

"I can't believe it. Aron? Did you tell him about us—how we live in Ripley now?" asked Marty.

"Course, I did. He said he wanted to come visit us sometime. In Canada, when he learned about the war, he wanted to come help fight to end slavery. He enlisted in the Black Brigade that built military fortifications and rifle pits to defend Cincy.

"He wanted to know about you, Amy. He asked if you became a teacher. I told him yes, but you hadn't been teaching lately because of the stir in Cincinnati."

"Did he tell you about his mother?" asked Mrs. Spencer.

"Yes, that's a long story. Sorry to say that she was captured by slave hunters right before she got to the crossing to Canada. When Aron got to Canada, 'course he couldn't find her, but some other Negro folks took him in. But there was a happy ending. She escaped, and in a few months, she was able to get to Canada and find him."

"Oh my, that is quite a story. I'm so happy that they were finally able to be together again."

The Spencers barely had time to enjoy Ed's company and be thankful that he had returned safely from his first brush with war when he announced that he was signing up as a "real soldier." He was joining the 113th Ohio Infantry Regiment. He would be mustered in at Camp Dennison near Cincinnati, for a period of three years.

Within a week, Virginia Spencer's hair turned from salt-and-pepper to snow white.

Thanksgiving 1862

Grace said before dinner was mostly a prayer for Ed's safety. Then, they tried to be cheerful, but soon each ate quietly, lost in their own solitary thoughts, eating delicious food, but not really savoring it. Dorothea had been invited, but she burst into tears when asked and said it would remind her too much of Ed's absence.

Marty asked if soldiers could send and receive mail. His father said yes, he thought they could.

"But how would we know where to send it?"

"We'll have to see what we can find out about mail," answered his father.

Then, Marty said something that nearly made them drop their faces into their plates.

"I wish I could go with him."

"Oh, no, Marty! You're needed here to help Seth and your father," his mother said.

Amy added, "I don't mean to be mean, but you know ... you've got a limp. You'd have trouble marching long distances..." She broke off and left the table sobbing. "I'm sorry... I just don't want you to go!" she practically shouted.

White-faced, her mother ran after her. They sat on the sofa and held each other while they cried.

Marty went to them and said, "Okay, you don't need to worry. I won't go. Not because of my limp, but because I'm needed here."

Mr. Spencer and Seth said they would clean the table and wash the dishes.

The pumpkin pie sat on the sideboard until later in the evening when they had all calmed down and began to make their way to the table again.

1863

On January 1, 1863, as the nation approached its third year of bloody civil war, President Lincoln issued the Emancipation Proclamation. The proclamation declared that all persons held as slaves within the rebellious states "are, and henceforward shall be free." The Spencer family rejoiced.

Aron

Marty was in the back work area sanding some lumber when Uncle Seth motioned to him to come to the front of the shop. A guy about his age, not quite as tall with a more solid build, stood there smiling at him. He wore a warm knit cap and a coat that didn't look heavy enough for the cold February day.

"Yes, may I help you?"

"Marty, it's me, Aron. Remember?" He removed his cap and revealed kinky hair, and Marty was immediately transported back to the ravine on that August day when they encountered slave hunters.

"I met Ed in Cincinnati when we were preparing for the possible attack. He told me that your family is now living in Ripley."

"Aron … yes, he told us he'd met you. I was surprised. I thought you were in Canada, and I'd never see you again. It's good to see you. Have a seat. I'll get my folks. Amy isn't here. She's teaching in Cincinnati."

"I've been staying in the Cincinnati area and wanted to see you and your family before I leave. I'm not sure whether I'll return to Canada right away or, if I could … I'd like to sign up for the Union Army, if they'll let me."

"You know that Ed joined in October?"

"Well, he told me he was thinking about it."

"Yeah, Mom and Amy are upset about it. Probably my father is too, but he doesn't say so. I'm stayin' here to help run the business."

Aron was invited to dinner, and the lively conversation with him lightened the gloom that shrouded the family since Ed left.

Aron told them about his life in Canada.

"I lived in a community called the Elgin Settlement. It was a community of Blacks in southern Ontario that was started by a minister named King who inherited several slaves and freed them, I think it was in 1849. It was also called Buxton, and the Buxton Mission that was supported by the Presbyterian Church. We had a church, a school, and a post office.

"Our school was so good, some white people sent their kids there." He glanced around the table with a sly look of amusement, and everyone laughed. "So, anyway, Amy will be happy to learn that I got a good education.

"A couple of years ago, two white slave catchers from the South—USA, that is—came to the area and spoke to a large crowd, trying to convince them that a slave boy named Joe was their property and they wanted to take him.

"Joe spoke up and said the men owned one of the biggest slave pens in the South. The crowd turned on the men and put them on the train. Joe had his freedom."

Aron spent the night and the following day, and one day lead into another. A comfortable cot was placed in Marty's room for him. He hung around Marty while he worked and soon began to help. Seth was pleased to find that he was an eager and careful worker.

∞∞∞

The first letter from Ed came from Franklin, Tennessee, not long after Aron arrived.

April 2, 1863

Dear family and Dorothea,
I'm only sending one letter. Let Dorothea know I'm ok and miss her.
Not much in the way of action yet. The dogwoods are blooming in the midst of war. Hope all of you are ok.

Ed

∞∞∞

Another night, Aron spoke with exuberance about the Emancipation Proclamation and told them about his mother's second escape from slavery.

"She came to Canada through a Pennsylvania route. She was rescued by a strong, determined Negro woman, whose name she later learned was Harriet Tubman.

"She delivered my mama to William Still, a free Negro who worked as a clerk for a Philadelphia society that worked to abolish slavery. He helped her get to Canada. It's said that he and Harriet Tubman helped hundreds of slaves to freedom. Harriet Tubman was nicknamed Moses, after the prophet in the Bible who led his people to freedom."

On weekends when Amy came home, she and Aron became good companions. They read together, and sometimes she read aloud while he listened. She recommended books to him. He said he hadn't read *Uncle Tom's Cabin*, although he'd heard about it. Marty suggested they read Frederick Douglass's autobiography.

One day, Marty walked into one of their reading sessions and said, "Well, it's almost like being back in the basement in Worthington."

Amy stuck her tongue out at him.

"Is that any way for a schoolteacher to act?" he teased. "What if one of your students saw you do that?"

"Oh, just go away!"

On May 22, 1863, the government authorized the formation of the United States Colored Troops. Aron signed up. He'd been waiting for this. The Spencers had grown fond of him and liked having him around. They were sad to see him go, especially sad because he was going to war, and they might never see him again.

Morgan's Raiders

After dinner, Mr. Spencer placed a box on the table.

"Any guesses to what's in it?" he asked the family.

"I think I know," said Marty. He had seen a similar box in John Parker's foundry, and Parker had shown him its contents.

"It's a pistol. Am I right?"

"Yes, you're right. Maybe I shouldn't ask how you know… Anyway, I want everyone to learn how to use it. By everyone, I mean Amy and, you too, Ginny." He always used the pet name "Ginny" when he was trying to persuade his wife of something. He knew that she viewed guns with revulsion.

"Morgan's raiders are in Ohio, and we need to protect ourselves." As an afterthought, he added, "It's the first time our state has been violated by Southern troops…"

"From what I hear, General John Hunt Morgan is a handsome gentleman with sky-blue eyes who doesn't want his men to mistreat women, and anyway, I doubt if he'd find our cabin. We're hidden here in the woods," Virginia Spencer said.

"Now Ginny," Luke Spencer said in a tone of gentle admonishment. "You never know. Tomorrow, we'll go outside, and everyone can learn how to use it and practice."

Unlike her mother, Amy was eager to learn how to use the pistol. She believed that women should learn things that were usually left to men.

∞∞∞

It was really happening—what the citizens of Ripley feared. Morgan's raiders were riding hard toward town. On July 14, Ripley prepared to meet the invaders.

Ripley folk hid their horses, their food, their keepsakes— anything they didn't want taken or destroyed. Mr. Spencer and Marty took two horses and hitched them to a tree in the woods.

People were jittery, some hurrying here and there, exchanging worried looks and trying not too successfully to put on a brave front and keep their fear in check. Others hunkered down in cellars, nearby woods, and other hiding places.

According to a scout, the raiders were two to three hundred in number. In Russellville, some ten miles away, they had looted stores and confiscated food and fresh horses. They'd threatened to burn a homestead if the owners didn't produce horses that they suspected were hidden.

Both Marty, his father, and Seth had signed onto a militia group that gathered just outside the town to fend off the marauders. John Parker was there, too. Their weapons included a large canon. The Ohio River, previously the everyday site of commercial and recreational activity, now had Union gunboats called tinclads, or ironclads—steamers that had been outfitted with protective iron. An ominous presence, they were trying to keep abreast of the raiders to prevent them from crossing the river into Kentucky.

People speculated about why Morgan had Ripley in his sights. Some thought he intended to lead his troops across the river here. Others said the entire operation was a feint to divert Union forces away from fighting the Rebs in crucial places. The direst speculation was that Morgan intended to wreak havoc on the town because of its reputation as a "hot bed of abolitionism."

But just as the siege of Cincinnati had been aborted so was the raid on Ripley. Maybe it was the presence of the gunboats or maybe Morgan knew the Ripley militia was ready for them.

Whatever the reasons, Morgan turned, and his army did not enter Ripley. There were several other skirmishes in Ohio, but on July 26, Union forces defeated the Raiders. Morgan surrendered in northeastern Ohio, near the Pennsylvania border. The captured enlisted men were sent to Camp Chase in Columbus, Ohio, or to other prison camps. Morgan and his officers were sent to the Ohio Penitentiary in Columbus.

Ed at War

The second letter came from Chickamauga, Georgia:

August 28, 1863

Dear family and Dorothea,

Just want you to know I'm alive and well. It is very hot in our uniforms in Georgia.

We are being issued new rifles, Spencer rifles that can get off 14 rounds per minute. Scary. Don't expect to use mine soon. Sorry, we are not allowed to say much about strategy.

We march to the song of "John Brown's Body."

Miss all of you. I only wrote one letter. Let Dorothea read this.

Love, Ed

∞∞∞

Though Luke Spencer had not found a group of friends as steady and amiable as those who met in Isaac's store in Worthington, he did find some acquaintances in Ripley. They shared information about the war, much of which Spence withheld from his wife and family. Photographs showing the aftermath of battles began to appear. They showed fallen men strewn out like animal carcasses, except dressed in blue or gray uniforms, or grotesque piles of mangled bodies, or severed limbs with their owners nowhere nearby.

One man had acquaintance with a soldier who had made a rare escape from the notorious Georgia confederate prison camp, Andersonville. The escapee himself was said to be nothing but skin and bones and required lengthy medical care. He brought tales of filth, malnutrition, and disease—scurvy, diarrhea, and dysentery. Cruelty was the rule. The officer who ran the prison was said to be proud of having so many "Federals" die under his charge.

Spence despaired that his son would not be alive at war's end, which didn't seem anywhere near. Still, he couldn't bring himself to sympathize with the Copperheads, or Peace Democrats, a movement that opposed the war and wanted an immediate settlement with the Confederates. Their leader, Clement L. Vallandigham, who served in the House of Representatives, called the war "wicked, cruel, and unnecessary" and accused President Lincoln of being a monarch, dubbing him "King Lincoln." In May 1863, he was put on trial for aiding and encouraging people to resist the government and was deported through enemy lines to the Confederacy. Still though, after Vallandigham's downfall, there were Copperheads around, ready to rear their heads when they thought they would not be heard by authorities. They believed that their leader had been deprived of his right to free speech.

Ed had the spunk and courage to join the Union army, so Spence supported the war that his son was fighting in. Besides, it seemed to Spence that ending the war would mean that the bloodshed thus far had been for naught. The Union would not be saved; the Confederacy would still be a separate entity. The Emancipation Proclamation would be nil. Slavery would continue.

The third letter came from Chickamauga:

September 1863

Dear family,

Survived battle of Chickamauga. It was terribul. Can't tell you how terribul. Rebs surprised and outnumbered us. Many killed and wounded. Makes me sick. I am lucky to be alive.

I miss everyone bad. I miss a normal life.

Love to all of you and Dorothea.

Ed

The Gettysburg Address

On November 19, Lincoln gave a powerful address at the dedication of the Gettysburg National Cemetery. Gettysburg had been the site of one of the war's deadliest battles. He spoke of "unfinished work" and the "great task remaining." In conclusion, he said:

> *... we here highly resolve that these dead shall not have died in vain— that this nation, under God, shall have a new birth of freedom—and that government of the people, by the people, for the people, shall not perish from the earth.*

1864

Frederick Douglass

In January 1864, Amy was invited by another teacher at her school to go hear a speech by Frederick Douglass. The speech was to be given before the Women's Loyal National League at the Cooper Institute in New York. Marty was envious.

When she returned, the family sat down to dinner, eager to hear about the talk. She described Douglass's physique as imposing and fierce with a broad forehead, prominent cheek bones, and dark piercing eyes. She said he had a fine head of bushy, grey-white hair, a mustache, and a beard. Also, he was very nicely dressed.

Amy characterized his speech as fine rhetoric, but so magnificent, she had difficulty following him at times.

Mr. Spencer commented, "So you mean he was wordy?"

"Well ... yes, you could say that."

"What was the gist of his message," asked Mrs. Spencer.

"Well ... I would say his message was that this war should be considered an Abolition war. He embraces the term that some Peace Democrats use in a derogatory way. He sees slavery as a moral issue worth fighting against... Wait a minute. I have a quote I wrote down. I'll get it..."

Amy returned to the table. "Okay, here it is,"

An Abolition war ... includes Union, Constitution,
Republican institutions, and all else that goes to make
up the greatness and glory of our common country.
On the other hand, exclude Abolition, and you exclude
all else for which you are fighting.

"Well, I can't say that I disagree with that statement," said Mr. Spencer. "I hear he'll be talking to President Lincoln … or maybe already has."

A Disturbing Letter

The fourth letter:

Dear Family,

Im sorry to tell you I was shot at the battle at Peach Tree Creek when we were trying to take Atlanta. A minié ball fractured the bone in my right leg just above the knee. I know you will think its awful but Im alive. The surgeon operated but didn't take my leg, not yet anyway. I fear infection.

We took Atlanta but our losses were heavy. I am thankful I did not get captured by the Rebs. Right now Im in a hospital in Atlanta. Its a hospital that was for Atlanta civilans. I know Sherman is going to move his troops out soon. Probly next month. I dont know what they will do with me. I cant soldier no more. I hope they dont leave me in this hospital.

Don't tell Dorothea about my leg.

Ed

The letter came not by postal service but by an anonymous messenger who knocked on the Spencer's door and didn't give his name. Mr. Spencer was pale and stern. Mrs. Spencer bowed her head and moaned, "I knew this war would ruin his life."

"No, Ginny, we don't know that yet. We'll do what we can to help him."

Amy was mute and teary-eyed.

Seth went outside and stared woodenly into the distance.

Marty secreted the letter from his father's desk and ran to see John Parker, who had stayed in Ripley to run his business and take care of his wife and children. He said he was contributing to the war by providing materials from his foundry.

He rushed into the foundry and pushed the letter toward Parker. Loudly, he declared, in a defiant voice, "I'm gonna go get him! Can you help steer me on a route? You've been to a lot of places … rescued a lot of slaves in the South…"

Parker read the letter and shook his head.

"Son … Martin … Marty … you don't know what you're getting' into! Georgia is Confederate territory, even if Sherman has captured Atlanta."

"If you don't want to help me, I'll just have to figure it out myself. I just gotta go try to get him. He'll be better off with his family."

"I don't know about you, boy. Fearless is what you are. Just give me a little time to think about this. Can you come back tomorrow? I need to talk to some people…"

Marty said OK, but he was so impatient and eager to do something that it was almost unbearable to wait. He wasn't thinking clearly, and he knew it and didn't care. He went home and put the letter back on his father's desk.

The next day, he went back to see Parker.

"Listen, Marty, I have a source who knows some things about the Union Army. Word is Sherman is going to move out of Atlanta in November after his army has a chance to rest and recoup. Ed might be sent to a Union Camp or even sent home."

"B-but … his leg. He can't walk very good. What if they leave him in Atlanta? Like you say, it's Confederate country. S-some Reb might kill him. He needs me … us to help him! I didn't fight in this war, but least I can do is help my brother."

"I figured you'd say that… well, my wife won't like it, but I'll see what we can do. I need another day…"

"I wouldn't want you to get hurt … take you away from your family, but I … we need to get goin'."

"My wife is used to my 'excursions'—she calls them. She knew every time I went to rescue a slave, I was in danger. She won't like it. Going into a war zone is different …

"Wait one more day. Come back tomorrow. I promise to have some plans."

Marty had had a knot in his stomach ever since he read Ed's letter. That night, after dropping into a restless sleep, he woke up suddenly, seized by a moment of terror. The knot had turned into a small, feral animal and moved up under his rib cage. It had a heart beating over his own heart. The danger and difficulty of his quest struck full force. Yet, he knew he had to do it.

The next day, John Parker had no more warnings of danger. Instead, he seemed coolheaded and confident. He had a plan. They would go by ship. He had arranged for them to board an ironclad.

"An ironclad!" Marty exclaimed. "How … how did you do that?"

"Well, I know a naval officer. I supply the Union Navy with materials I make in my foundry."

Before he left, Parker gave him a haversack that contained a knife and two small flasks. He said one would be for water, the other held whiskey. Marty was surprised at the whiskey. "Why do I need that? I don't drink whiskey."

"Well, son, you never know when you might be in a situation in which whiskey might be a good barter for something. Also, if Ed's in pain, well, sips of whiskey might help. Don't take much else. You don't want to lug around a heavy haversack … maybe a change of clothes. On second thought, put on two layers of clothing and some long underwear. It'll keep you warm, and if the top layer gets dirty, you can just take those clothes off." He paused. "Have you got a pistol?"

"My pa has one."

"Is it heavy?"

"Not too."

"You know how to use it?"

"Yes, my father taught the whole family to use it."

"If you can, I advise you to bring it … with extra ammunition."

On the Ohio River

Parker and a sailor named Kent rowed their canoe to the ironclad, or tinclad, as the ships were sometimes called. There, a rope ladder was extended, and they climbed onto the ship.

If it had not been for his worries about Ed and the perilousness of their mission, Marty would have thought of it as a grand adventure. He'd seen ironclads from afar mostly when they shadowed Morgan's Raiders trying to prevent them from crossing the river into Kentucky. Though they were man-made and powered by steam, they seemed otherworldly—like leviathans that rose from the deep. Amy had told him about a book about a sea captain named Ahab who pursued a great white whale named Moby Dick. The whale had eventually destroyed the captain and his ship. Marty thought to himself that his private name for the ironclad would be Moby Dick. He would just disregard the destruction part of the tale.

Rather than tell his family he was leaving, he left a note on his father's desk while he was taking an after-lunch nap. He felt like he'd taken the coward's way out, but he just couldn't face their questions and anxieties about his safety.

Aboard the tinclad, John Parker told him they should be quiet and stay mostly in the area assigned to them, so as not to get in the crew's way. To help Marty adjust to this new experience, Parker schooled Marty on nautical terms.

"Do you know where the stern of the ship is located?"

"Not sure—the front maybe."

"Nope, that's the bow. Sometimes, people say stem instead of bow. Stern means the rear of the ship. There's a saying you've probably heard, 'from stem to stern.'"

"Yeah, I think I've heard that."

"Aft means near the stern. Some other terms are port that means left of the bow; starboard is right of the bow."

Then, Parker told Marty about the route he had planned. They would debark the tinclad at Paducah, Kentucky, the confluence of the Ohio and Tennessee Rivers. Then, they would board a paddle steamer to take them on the Tennessee River to Chattanooga, Tennessee, which was near the Georgia border. Parker had arranged through contacts for a man with a wagon and team of horses to take them overland to Atlanta.

Their conversation was interrupted by a sailor who introduced himself as Petty Officer Larson. He wanted to show them the part of the ship where they'd spend most of their time. It was called the berth deck and was devoted to the crew. Like the crew, they would sleep in hammocks that were stored when not in use.

Then, he offered to give them a short tour of the ship.

They saw the galley, or kitchen, the captain's cabin, and the stateroom that housed the officers. Larson pointed out the circular windows in the deck that supplied light to the interior of the vessel. He said iron covers were placed over the openings when going into battle. At night and on overcast days, lanterns and candles were used. Then, the engine room, which held the engine, boilers, pumps, and ventilation blowers. Most fascinating to Marty was the revolving turret where the big guns were mounted. Its revolutions allowed firing in different directions. Marty was in awe of the mechanical artistry of the ship. He thought maybe he should have been a sailor.

At 5 p.m., they were invited to eat with the crew. The meal was salt pork and beans; the dessert was a dish they called "duff," a boiled pudding of flour and water, sweetened with molasses with chopped, dried apples in it. Marty felt shy sitting amid the swaggering seamen, who weren't shy about asking them questions. They were curious as to why Northerners who were not soldiers were going South. They directed the question toward him, but when he hesitated to reply, Parker answered. He was somewhat evasive, saying they were going to Paducah to pick up Marty's brother who had been injured in the war. One sailor asked if Marty had been in military service or were going to join. He told them that he had stayed home to take care of his family and help run their business.

It dawned on Marty that they did not direct questions to Parker, probably because he was a Black man. It was a shock to realize that they regarded him as the leader and Parker as his helper. Of course, this was in a sense, true, because he had asked Parker for help, but Parker's knowledge and connections were the vital elements in this journey. He had begun to realize the folly of his threat to make the trip on his own and felt bad about the indignity Parker might feel.

The ship had been quiet in the afternoon, but it came alive in the evening. After a call to quarters for inspection, the men were at leisure. Two musicians brought out a banjo and a fiddle and began playing lively tunes. Two men danced jigs and were rewarded with claps, stomps, and cheers. A group of men improvised a square dance, linking arms with their elbows as they skipped around a circle. Some men were playing cards or dominos or throwing dice. Parker told Marty they were probably gambling, which was against regulations, but there were no officers around to enforce the rules. When he'd watched the tinclads patrolling the river during Morgan's raid, Marty would never have dreamed that such activity would take place on the ships.

One older, garrulous sailor started a conversation with them about Paducah. He asked Marty if his brother had been injured in the big battle that took place in March. Imitating Parker's previous evasiveness, Marty replied, "Er, we're not sure."

"Well, here's what happened. Paducah was under Union control, even though it was a Confederate-sympathizing town. A Confederate general named Forrest led a raid on it, mainly it's said to get supplies for his army. The Union army under

Colonel Hicks was hit by surprise and outnumbered. They holed up in Fort Anderson.

"There was gun boats involved to support Hicks's troops. I wasn't on neither of them, but I know a man who was. The gun boats' fire did a lot of damage. They cleared the cavalry from the streets.

"Forrest demanded that Hicks surrender, but Hicks refused. Both sides lost several men. The Confederates ransacked the city to take horses and supplies. After they withdrew, Hicks ordered several houses burned because he heard that Forrest's troops might come back… You'll find a town that's seen a lot of destruction when you get to Paducah."

After his restless night at home the evening before, Marty was tired. He liked sleeping in the hammock. The gentle lull of the ship put him into a restful sleep.

He nearly fell out of the hammock at 5 a.m. when a bugler sounded reveille. The sailors immediately got up and started rolling up their hammocks for storage. So, that's what Parker and Marty did, too. They hastened to get out of the way when the crew started swabbing the berth deck.

Later in the day, Parker mentioned the sailor's account of the battle of Paducah and the fact that the townspeople supported the South.

"Kentuck' is a border state. There are many that favor the South, even though the official government is Unionist. Both Abe Lincoln and Jefferson Davis hail from Kentuck'. That'll tell you somethin'," he told Marty. "It didn't secede, but slavery was allowed."

The state of Kentucky was of great interest to Parker because he had made many forays in and through it, sometimes experiencing close shaves with slave owners or slave hunters.

"When the war began, Uncle Abe asked the Kentuck' governor to supply troops. He refused because he was a

Southern sympathizer. But the legislature was Unionist, so the result was a declaration of neutrality.

"Which both sides have violated. There have been battles. Supporters of the South even set up a shadow government. As far as I know, it didn't do much."

Marty remembered sitting on the bench with Dan, gazing across the river. It had seemed so peaceful on the opposite shore. It was easy to be lulled into temporary forgetfulness of the people trying to escape bondage and the men hunting them—the violent clashes that occurred between the hunters and the hunted, or between the hunters and the people helping the hunted. It was hard to believe that these conflicts led to a nationwide civil war in which thousands of men were dying. A war his own brother had joined and paid a high price for— the major injury of a limb.

∞∞∞

The tinclad docked at Paducah. The crew was in good spirits because they could go ashore for a few hours. Petty Officer Larson, who had kept them under his wing, stayed with them a while and showed them a city scarred by war. Confederate troops had burned a hospital, glass works, and several other buildings before abandoning the city. It was the first time Marty had seen the destruction of war. He regarded it soberly, fighting off a feeling of despondency. He thought about the cabin his family had built and his parents' delight in it. People build structures and take pride in them. Then, other people destroy them.

Before taking his leave, Larson showed them a bakery he liked. When they entered, the aroma of fresh-baked bread was so mouth-watering that Marty felt transported to his mother's kitchen. They bought two loaves of bread and some pastries for dessert. Parker asked the waitress if they had any hard tack. She disappeared into a back room and brought back a bag. He asked if she had any more, and she disappeared once more. He bought two bags which he said they might need to sustain them on their journey.

The Road to Atlanta

The paddle wheeler had been adapted as a gun boat, but a sailor told them it was unlikely that there would be any gunfire from the shore. The Union controlled the area. They felt safe enough to be on the deck as the boat steamed toward Chattanooga.

Chattanooga had also seen major battles. Unlike Paducah, the Union Army had been the aggressor. Parker knew some things about Chattanooga. He said he'd been there once a long time ago. It was a vital railroad junction, and the Union invaded it to begin their march into Georgia. The major battles had taken place on Missionary Ridge and Lookout Mountain.

They made their way across the city until they came to a foundry, a place that Parker knew of through his business. He had arranged for them to meet a man who had a wagon and horse and would take them to Atlanta. On a bench outside the foundry, an older grizzled, colored man sat dozing, Parker touched his shoulder to wake him.

"John Parker here. Are you Samuel?"

"Huh? Yuh, I'm Samuel." He looked at them with bleary eyes. "You're Parker—and who is this?" He gestured toward Marty.

"Martin Spencer. His brother, Ed, is a Union soldier."

"How comes youse not fightin', too?" Samuel demanded.

Parker answered for him. "He had to stay in Ohio and run the family business and take care of his family."

Marty started to say that he didn't run the business, just helped his uncle and Ed, but Parker had moved on to the business at hand.

"Where are your horses and wagon?"

Samuel jerked his thumb to a grove of trees. "Got 'em over there just in case . . . somebody might steal 'em, you know."

They walked to the place. Marty could tell that Parker was chagrined by what he saw. A look passed over his face that belied his usual confidence.

Instead of horses, there was only one old swaybacked mule, and the wagon, too, had seen its better days, though it did have a makeshift cover that appeared sturdy enough.

For the first time, Marty felt uneasy about the quest they were on. One of his mother's sayings came to mind, "a fool's errand." But then he had an image of Ed, stricken and helpless, and looked at Parker with a silent plea.

Almost in response, Parker recovered his aplomb. "You think this old mule can get us to Atlanta?" he asked with a smile.

"Don't go insultin' Benjamin here. He's got a few years on him, but he's plenty sturdy." He paused and looked saddened. "See, I had a good mare ... but a Reb took her, one of General Bragg's men, when they was routed by Sherman's army. They would've took Benjamin, too, but he stalled, and the man didn't have no patience... Sometimes, it pays to be stubborn, don't it, Ben?" He stroked the mule's head. "Only one thing ... Benjamin got his own pace—slow but sure."

"We best be goin' then. It's mid-mornin'."

Benjamin plodded along. He was slow but seemed determined to get them to wherever they wanted to go. The road was rough and rutted in some places, but dry weather helped make it travelable. They could see that armies had worn it and the surrounding fields down. There were frequent piles of horse manure that Benjamin usually managed to evade. Samuel was mostly silent, sometimes dozing off for brief periods in the wagon seat and letting Benjamin lead the way. The first time it happened, Parker looked alert, as though he were ready to grab the reins, if need be. But Benjamin was so steady that Parker relaxed and appeared amused at Samuel's naps.

They encountered a few travelers, most of whom seemed to be local farmers. Once, they heard the hooves of horsemen in the distance, and Parker told Marty to hide under some raggedy blankets in the wagon.

"Wouldn't want any soldiers to question why a man your age isn't wearing blue or questioning if you might be a Reb."

The riders were three soldiers in Union blue who paid them scant attention. They seemed bent on reaching their destination and left the wagon in their dust.

"They goin' to Atlanta," said Samuel, as if he knew for sure.

Mid-afternoon, they came to the Georgia-Tennessee border which was marked by a weathered sign. Samuel pulled the reins to the left to guide the wagon into a copse of maple trees.

"Benjamin is thirsty and hungry," Samuel announced. He got a large jug of water from the wagon and poured some into a pan for Benjamin and some into a cup for himself.

"Y'all want some?"

"We've got some in our flasks. Better save yours," said Parker.

Samuel found a sack of oats and put some in another pan for the mule.

Parker got out the hard tack and offered some to Samuel.

On the road again, Georgia stretched before them with its red clay hills and sandy terrain. They passed small farms with nondescript houses and occasionally, saw stately, pillared mansions situated a distance down a road lined with canopied oak trees.

"Bet the Union Army helped themselves to all the crops on the way to Atlanta," said Parker.

"Course they did," said Samuel.

As the trip wore on, Parker tried to engage the reticent Samuel in conversation.

"You live in Atlanta, right?"

"Just outside."

"Were you in the city when the Rebs knew they were losing it to the Yanks?"

"Yep, shore was. My massah done let me go a week befo'. I hightailed it to the city."

"What was it like … when the Confederate Army knew Sherman was going to take the city?"

"People puttin' they valubles in wagons and takin' 'em to the country. My 'pinion is the Yanks will still get 'em anyway. Threw open the warehouse and gives all the food away—flour, corn, sorghum, ham, bacon, sweet taters, tobaccy, everthing. See dem sacks back there," he motioned to the back of the wagon. "I done hep myself. Some people lootin', takin' what ain't theirs. I don't take nothin' 'cept what the warehouse give me."

"Did the Confederate Army destroy things so the Feds couldn't get them?"

"Yep, shore did. First, they try to take ammo to Macon. Loaded the cars and hooked 'em to the *General* and the *Missouri*. They run into the Feds and had to back 'em up all the way back to Atlanta, Then they burn, blow things up—the train engines and cars. Poured tar on 'em and set 'em on fire. Ear-splittin'—pop, boom, pop goin' all night. Sky lit up like hot sun. Some drunk soljers set fire to houses, too."

"The *General* and the *Missouri* are engines?"

"Yep, they was mighty fine ones, too. A shame."

"What was it like when the Yanks arrived?"

"A few Rebs had guns and snuck 'round and tried to kill some soljers. They's rounded up pretty quick. Some people glad to see the Yanks. Not all colored folk neither. Some Yankee soljers looted, but not so much as you might think.

Now, they's camped everwhere—even on the park 'round city hall. Some took over people's houses."

Marty was getting an earful of what war was all about.

They met elderly, colored man walking down the road carrying a basket. Samuel stopped to talk to him. "I'm a free man," the man announced. "Yankees done come through here and freed all us colored folks."

"Y'all goin' to Atlanta?" he asked.

"Yup," answered Samuel.

"Well, good luck to yuh. General Sherman done took control of the city."

"Yup, we knows."

Then, the man reached into his basket and gave each of them some pecans.

They traveled until the sun went down and stopped at a spring. It wasn't by accident. Samuel seemed to know the spring was there.

"We can rest here … get some sleep and should reach Atlanta by tomorrow," Samuel told them.

"Will we cross Peachtree Creek?"

"I spec so," answered Samuel. "What you know about Peachtree Creek?"

"That's where my brother Ed was wounded and taken prisoner."

"Oh, my, my, I unnerstand."

Parker thought they should take turns staying awake. "We should be on guard … you just never know …"

Marty said he wasn't sleepy yet, so he would take the first watch. It was an eerie feeling being in a forest with only a half moon giving some light. He was aware of animal sounds around him—an owl hooting and something scratching as if rooting for food. Once, he sensed a presence and looked out of the wagon to see a racoon. He felt around in his haversack and found a hardtack biscuit Parker had given him. He tossed it to the raccoon.

Parker sat up alert. "What you doin'?"

"Just gave a coon a hardtack."

"We might need that food ourselves, boy."

Marty wondered if Parker had really been asleep. Maybe he had dozed. He thought of the past exploits Parker had told him about. He'd had to find his way through dark woods, pursued by slave hunters. He supposed that Parker had survived because he was able to stay awake and alert.

Early the next morning, Samuel built a small campfire and boiled them some coffee and oats, which they ate with hard tack and the pecans the colored man had given them.

They came to Peachtree Creek. The water seemed too high to cross. Samuel said it might be shallower upstream, so they traveled a bit, and he was right. Marty looked at Parker questioningly, thinking maybe he would say it wasn't safe. But Parker had a poker face, and Marty trusted him. They got to the middle and Benjamin stopped. Samuel started talking to him in almost a crooning voice.

"C'mon, Ben. You's a good boy. You can do it. You can get us across." The mule lapped some water and shook his head.

"C'mon, Ben, you's so handsome and strong. Can you get us across this darn crick?"

And, finally, Ben started moving.

Ben balked again when they entered the area where there were palisades and trenches built by the Confederate Army when they were defending Atlanta. Samuel said that Atlantans had forced their slaves to construct two rings of fortifications around the city. He had somehow escaped that labor. Samuel had to get off the wagon seat and lead him around the obstacles. They saw Union troops stationed ahead, and Parker told Marty to hide under the blankets.

"They probably won't give two colored people any trouble." He was right. They told them to be careful, and they moved on.

"Somewhere near here is where Gen'ral McPherson got killed. He was young and Gen'ral Sherman favored him, so they say," Samuel commented.

Atlanta

"**A**tlanta was once a bootiful city," Samuel said, as they entered the heart of Atlanta.

Now, it lay in devastation. Many buildings were in ruins or had gaping holes and missing windows. The acrid smell of burned tar assaulted their nostrils, and the air was hazy with smoke. Amidst the destruction, they saw soldiers in blue uniforms strolling the streets, talking and laughing. A few grim-faced civilians showed themselves, even though the Confederate leader, General Hood, had told everyone to leave when the army evacuated. Samuel said General Sherman also issued orders for citizens to leave. He said some people who stayed claimed to be loyal to the Union cause and might have to prove it.

He pointed at an official-looking building. "Tha's the courthouse with the Union flag flyin' above it."

Union encampments surrounded the courthouse and dotted the city. Many were wooden structures that had been built from materials of razed buildings. Covered wagons that held supplies for the army and served as temporary medical facilities for the sick and wounded lined up on Decatur and Peach Tree Streets. Some buildings were intact though pock-marked by shells, *The Intelligencer* newspaper building being one. Marty winced when he saw a business with the sign, "Auction and Negro Sales." It had never occurred to him that the business of selling Negroes would be advertised so openly, just like selling food or clothing or furniture or other everyday things.

They found a stable where Samuel could house Benjamin, who got royal treatment from his owner's grooming and rubdowns. Marty sat on a stool near Benjamin's stall or napped in the wagon. Samuel told him some things about his life. He'd belonged to a man who treated him well, that is, he gave him food and shelter and didn't beat him, but he sold Samuel's only son when the boy was only ten years old. "My wife, she couldn't stand it no mo' after dat. She done hang herself with a sheet she stole from the mistress's bed."

"I's goin' to look for him, but I don' know if I would even know him. Ain't dat awful—not to recognize your own son?"

Marty agreed it was awful. He thought of Mr. Shelby in *Uncle Tom's Cabin*, who was considered a "good" slave owner but had wanted to sell Eliza and George Harris's young son, Harry, to settle his debts. It was a book that shocked him when Amy read it. He now realized how much it portrayed reality.

They found a place where they could have a campfire and cook some pork and beans for dinner. Samuel told them another story. He said he had once visited the town of Millen with his master. Nearby was a Confederate prison camp called Camp Lawton. While his master and his wife stayed with relatives a few days, Samuel had gone to the camp and asked if they had any temporary jobs he could do for pay. He wanted to earn some money in the hope of buying his freedom. They let him in and gave him a shovel to start digging a hole. "Da's wanted it real big." When one of the prisoners told him the guards were going to use it as a mass grave for Union prisoners, Samuel left without finishing the job and collecting his pay.

Marty was eager to find a hospital and look for Ed, but Parker told him to lay low for a day or two, while he did some recon.

The evening of the second day, Parker returned to their camp with a Yankee uniform. He didn't say where or how he got it. "Try it on," he told Marty. "It looks like it will fit pretty well."

"Why should I wear it?"

"Well, we're here to get Ed. We don't want someone to conscript you in the army. Tomorrow, you can go to a hospital, pretending to be a Union soldier looking for your brother."

Parker told them the political talk was that President Lincoln was sure to be re-elected because of Sherman's success in Atlanta.

During the siege, the Atlanta hospitals had been ordered to evacuate. Their equipment was loaded onto railroad cars and taken south. The Union Army was setting up makeshift facilities, using some of the buildings that had previously been used for Atlanta citizens and injured Confederate soldiers. First, they tried the site of the former Receiving and Distributing Hospital.

Marty was nervous about being an impostor, but he swallowed hard and did it. A nurse agreed to accompany him as he passed by beds holding maimed and disfigured soldiers. It was hard to bear.

"What is your brother's name? We have a list of occupants, but, of course, it's not complete."

"Ed … Edward Spencer."

She did not find his name on the roster.

"There are other sites … or maybe he was released to an encampment."

The next day, they found a site at the fairgrounds that had been a hospital and repeated the search. But again, he did not find Ed.

Marty felt discouraged and dispirited. If Ed had been taken to an encampment, how would they ever find him. A worse thought was that his brother was dead.

"We can't give up yet," said Parker. He had made acquaintance with some of the Union sympathizers who had stayed in the city. One woman who said her brother was a Union soldier told him that she thought the Atlanta Medical College building was used as a hospital.

And there they found him. He was sleeping, and Marty stood beside his bed watching him. His entire being was flooded with relief.

Ed opened his eyes tentatively at first, but then wide with disbelief. "How can you be here? I must be dreaming."

"No," Marty said. "You're not dreaming. John Parker and I came all the way from Ripley to find you after we got your letter."

"That just don't seem possible."

"Well, we did it."

"Why are you in blue? You didn't join, did you?"

"Nope. It's sort of a disguise." He clapped Ed on the shoulder. "Listen, I got to go tell Parker I found you and see if we can get you out of here. Do you think you can stand … with help, I mean?"

Ed threw off the cover and showed a heavily bandaged leg. "I think I can manage. Could you find me some crutches?"

"I'll see."

"You're not going to be the only one in the family with a limp. And, oh yes, Bone has a limp, too." He grinned at Marty, and Marty managed to respond with a grin that felt more like a grimace.

Outside, he sat on a bench and said a prayer of thanks that he'd found his brother. He felt undone—by Ed's injury, by the stricken, occupied city of Atlanta, by all the death and destruction the war had wrought.

Later, he and Parker went looking for crutches but couldn't find any that were not in use. Finally, Parker said, "I'll make some." He got some lumber from a pile of rubble and began carving with the knife he always carried.

Waylaid

His eyes flew open. He caught a glimpse of gray as a strong arm gripped his neck.

He'd been dozing on a bluff near the wagon while Parker and Samuel were down by the creek. Samuel had unharnessed Benjamin to let him drink. Ed was asleep in the wagon.

Two men in Confederate uniforms had jumped him. They took his pistol and now aimed it at him.

He wasn't as scared as he was upset that he had let his group down. He hadn't been watchful.

He was relieved that he had shed the Yankee uniform for his regular clothes. Now, he desperately needed to keep the men from finding Ed who *was wearing his Yankee jacket.*

The men were rifling through his haversack that he'd laid on the ground beside him. They found some hardtack and the flask of whiskey.

One of them examined the pistol to see how many shots were in the chamber.

"You got more ammo for this pistol?" he demanded of Marty.

"Nuh … no … used it all," he lied. He'd hidden some under a bag of flour in the wagon.

"We got lucky, Billy. Two slaves and a boy with a pistol," said the man who was named Jeb.

"And food! Must be food in this wagon, I'm hongry. I want hot food, not this hardtack shit," said Billy. He started to climb in the wagon.

"Wait! Here comes Samuel. He's a good cook. Let him find some vittles and cook for you," Marty said.

Parker was scrambling up the bank. Samuel followed, leading Benjamin.

"We don't care if Sherman done freed you. I got bullets here with your names on them. It says you my slaves, and I want you to cook us some real food," ordered Jeb.

"We got some sweet potatoes and salt pork in the wagon. I'll start a fire," Samuel complied. He climbed into the wagon to get the food and managed to make sure Ed was covered by blankets.

Marty felt strangely calm. He watched Parker. He remembered Parker's tales of derring-do when he was rescuing slaves in Kentucky. He was confident that he would get them out of this predicament. He wasn't carrying his haversack, and Marty wasn't sure where he'd put his pistol. It wasn't in a holster around his waist as it usually was when he strode down the middle of the street in Ripley. It must be in the wagon.

Jeb opened the flask, smelled it, took a swig, and gave a big sigh of satisfaction. He passed it to his companion.

"Whiskey, Billly boy. Real whiskey. I ain't had none since we left Chattanooga."

Parker helped Samuel with the cooking. He asked the soldiers why they were separated from their regiment.

"Now, I don't see how that's any of your bizness. We just got lost, didn't we, Billy?"

"Yep, that's pretty much what happened."

They took turns sipping the whiskey. They, too, watched Parker sharply. No matter if Parker adopted a twang and Negro dialect. No matter if Parker acted subservient, there was an aura about him that said he wasn't.

They ate until they were satiated and then asked if there was more whiskey. "I'll get it, Massah," Parker said looking at Marty. He climbed in the wagon to get the whiskey. Marty was sure he'd manage to get his gun, but Jeb stood by the wagon, aiming the pistol at him and watching his every move

Parker leaned out of the wagon and dropped his haversack on the ground. Billy grabbed it and pulled out the flask.

As they drank the whiskey, they became talkative.

"Where you from, boy?" Jeb asked Marty.

"My folks own a plantation not far from heah."

"What you'all doin' heah?"

"We needed some watah from the crick."

Parker gave Marty a sly glance.

With his stomach full and the whiskey dulling his senses, Billy seemed ready to nod off.

Jeb slapped his arm. "We can't sleep yet. We got to travel. Bet you, he hides whiskey from his old man, so he can nip it on the side." He gestured toward Marty. "What do yuh think, Billy?"

"I think I gotta go to the woods …"

Billy got up and disappeared in the woods, apparently to relieve himself, while Jeb sat with the pistol aimed at them.

When Billy returned, Jeb asked, "Yuh think I should just shoot'm, Billy? We fought 'side boys younger'n him. He oughta be with the army."

"Nah. He can walk home with the slaves. We'll take the wagon and the mule."

Jeb ordered Samuel to harness Benjamin.

He climbed onto the wagon seat, while Billy, obviously unsteady now, climbed into the back of the wagon.

Jeb shook the reins and ordered him to gitty up. Benjamin refused to move.

"Ain't you got no whip for this mule?"

Samuel shook his head no.

Jeb climbed down and found a good-sized limb. He got back on the wagon seat and started hitting Benjamin on the rump.

Benjamin snorted and bared his teeth but didn't move.

"Where's that old Sambo that takes care of the mule?" he demanded of Marty.

Samuel had disappeared into the woods. He wanted no part of trying to get Benjamin to move.

"Billy, get your ass out of the wagon and hep me get this mule movin'."

But Billy was out cold. When Jeb was preoccupied with Benjamin, he'd gotten careless. In one swift move, Parker, lithe as a cougar, had jumped into the back of the wagon, pinned Billy down, held his knife to his throat, and knocked him unconscious.

A shot rang out and Jeb fell off the wagon seat screaming. The bullet that hit him in the shoulder came from Parker's pistol, but it was Ed who pulled the trigger.

Parker had given it to him before he'd gone to the creek.

They lifted Billy out of the wagon and put him on the ground. Parker grabbed Marty's pistol and threw Jeb an old blanket to wrap his wound. Finally, Parker tossed him a bag of hardtacks.

Samuel was back from the woods and in the wagon seat. He shook the reins, and Benjamin took off at a faster pace than he'd ever done the entire trip.

"They were deserters," Parker said.

Parker estimated they had about 70 miles to go before they'd be back in Chattanooga, where they'd take a paddle wheeler to Paducah and then board an ironclad to travel on the Ohio River to go home to Ripley.

Going Home

By the time they reached Chattanooga, Ed was in a lot of pain. Parker said they should find a military doctor to look at him.

The doctor looked at his wound, and said that he saw no signs of infection, but that it would take a long time to heal. He gave him a morphine injection, like he'd received in the Atlanta hospital.

Parker and Marty asked Samuel to go with them. They said he would like Ripley. But Samuel said, "No, Georgia is my home. And what would Benjamin do without me? Also, I got plans to search for my son farther South." He said he might come to visit them sometime when the war was over.

On the tinclad, Ed was treated as a hero. Some sailors thought he wouldn't be comfortable sleeping in a hammock, so they found a cot for him, with an extra pillow so that he could rest his leg on it if he wanted.

Parker managed to send a message ahead to the Spencer family that they were on their way. "Wouldn't want you to just walk in the door with no warning. Might give someone a heart attack," he said.

When the boat docked, they could see all the Spencers and their Uncle Seth standing on the shore smiling and waving. Ed and Marty looked at each other and blinked away tears.

Dorothea wasn't there, but Marty would bet that his mother had told her about Ed's injury, even though Ed had said not to tell her. Marty knew Ed felt self-conscious and uncertain about how his injury would affect her. He hoped, no, he was sure, all would be well between them eventually.

There were hugs all around and thanks to John Parker for his help. No recriminations for Marty for his abrupt disappearance on a dangerous mission.

Ed was unnervingly quiet the first two weeks at home. Mrs. Spencer and Amy fretted and asked Marty repeatedly if he thought Ed was okay.

Mr. Spencer scolded, "Leave him be! He's been through hell. He's got a serious injury to show for it. You can't just expect him to step back into home life like nothin' happened."

Marty told his family about the trip on "Moby Dick," the trek across Georgia with Samuel and Benjamin, and the desecration of Atlanta. He omitted the story of being waylaid by Confederate deserters. Maybe someday when enough time had passed, he would tell them.

The family told him they'd had a short note from Aron not long ago. He was somewhere in Virginia.

Mrs. Spencer and Amy had kept Dorothea informed about Ed. After he'd been home about three weeks, she came to see him. She'd wanted to come sooner, but Ed said, "I need some time to sort things out in my mind."

After her visit, Ed brightened and began to talk more. One day, he went into the furniture workshop and, laying his crutches to the side, started to sand a table. He began to work a little every day. His pain lessened, but he still relied on morphine injections given by a local doctor, who advised him to taper his dependence on them.

Thanksgiving, 1864

Marty drove Ed to Dorothea's house to have dinner with her family.

John Parker showed up with a sweet potato pie his wife had made. The Spencers invited him to eat with them, but he declined, saying he was having dinner with his family.

They talked of the war, a topic often avoided when Ed was there. There had been much speculation about Sherman's strategy after Atlanta. On November 15, he put it to rest when his army began marching south, leaving Atlanta smoking and in ruins.

"You think Atlanta was in ruins when you saw it?" Mr. Spencer addressed Marty.

"According to newspaper reports, Sherman ordered about half of it burned before he started South. He burned manufacturing companies and anything the Rebs might use in the war. He also destroyed all of the railroads north of the city that brought supplies to his army, so the South can't use them."

At the end of the meal, Marty told them about the business in Atlanta with the sign that read "Auction and Negro Sales." He said he was thankful that his parents had reared him to be an abolitionist.

1865

War's End

General Sherman's army had ended their march to the sea by taking Savannah. Then the army moved north to the Carolinas. After they defeated the Confederate Army in March at the battle of Bentonville, people thought that victory was imminent for the Union Army. And, indeed, this was the case. On April 6, the nation's long national nightmare came to an end when General Robert E. Lee surrendered to General Ulysses S. Grant at the home of Wilmer McLean following the last major battle of the Civil War, the Battle of Appomattox Court House.

Thanksgiving 1865

On this Thanksgiving Day, there was much to be thankful for. Ed's leg injury was improving. Most of the time, he used a cane instead of crutches. He and Dorothea announced that they planned to marry in the spring.

Aron had returned from the war safely and was living with the Spencers temporarily while he thought about what he wanted to do next.

But the joy and optimism were tempered by sorrow for the great losses the country had suffered and by the death of President Lincoln. He was shot in the back of the head as he sat watching a play in Ford's Theatre in Washington, D.C. The assassin John Wilkes Booth, an actor and Confederate sympathizer, was hunted down and shot by a Union soldier a few days later.

Amy said grace, and they concentrated on appreciation for the meal before them. The mood was reflective and the conversation mostly fitful small talk.

Once, Mr. Spencer commented he'd heard that General John Hunt Morgan had been killed.

"He and his officers were imprisoned in the Ohio Penitentiary, but a few months later, they escaped by using kitchen knives to tunnel their way through an airshaft. They returned to the Confederate Army, but then, Morgan met his Maker when a Union soldier shot him last year. Remember the turmoil when they rode toward Ripley, and everyone prepared for an invasion?"

After a choice of apple or pumpkin pie for dessert, people became more energized when Aaron began to talk about his war experiences. Though he'd been staying with the Spencers for a week, he hadn't talked about the war much, beyond saying that he was happy to have survived. He'd busied himself with helping with furniture-making and said he enjoyed the work.

"I had a particular place I wanted to volunteer to fight," he said. "That was in South Carolina, particularly the coastal islands. See, I'd heard that Harriet Tubman was there. She was helping slaves who had been freed by the Union Army but had no money or skills to survive on their own. Remember she was the person who led my mama to freedom? I wanted to meet her, and I figured that anything she was involved in was worthwhile.

"I did meet her, and she remembered my mama. She said she remembered all the dozens of people she'd led out of slavery, even though she had headaches from a head injury she'd suffered when she was young.

"You might think she'd be a big, strong woman, considering the things she's done--tramping and hiding in the woods and swamps--but she's short, around 5 feet tall, I'd say. Maybe being short helped her hide from slave hunters. But, of course, she is strong even though she's short. She's also tough and always carried a gun. I heard that she threatened to use it on any slaves who got cold feet and wanted to return to the plantations she rescued them from. She always had a head wrap and wore loose pants she called 'bloomers.'

"She was a spy who learned where the Confederate torpedoes were located and helped the Union Army raid and destroy several large plantations along the Combahee River. I was in the group of Black men who followed her. We also freed and rescued many slaves during the raid.

"Did you know that she knew John Brown and may have helped recruit some people for his raid on Harper's Ferry? John Brown called her 'General Tubman.'

"The last time I talked to her, she told me to come visit her after the war was over. She said she knew I would survive."

Aron's story was so vivid and powerful that everyone just sat quietly for a while.

Finally, Amy asked, "Are you going to do that ... visit Harriet Tubman?"

"Yes, I am. I'm not sure when, maybe I'll wait until next spring when the weather is warmer."

∞∞∞

After Ed and Dorothea's wedding in April, Aron left for Auburn, New York, to visit Harriet Tubman. The Spencers heard from him in July. He said that he was returning to Canada to visit his mother and friends for a while.

Aron returned to Ripley in early fall and resumed helping in the furniture shop. Seth Porter offered to pay him for his labor, but he said he'd work for room and board. He was learning a lot about the furniture-making business and was thinking about starting his own business in Auburn.

PART III:
POSTBELLUM
(1866)

1866

Thanksgiving

At dinner's end, Amy stood up and looked around the table like she was in her classroom ready to teach a lesson.

"I have an important announcement."

Her parents thought maybe she was going to announce her engagement to the Cincinnati teacher who had been courting her. They had met him once and liked him well enough. He seemed like a serious person who would be a good match for her.

"I should say *we* have an announcement."

She glanced at Aron who had been uncharacteristically quiet. Mrs. Spencer wondered if he knew that Amy was going to announce her engagement, and he would miss his close relationship with her.

Then, he stood up and cleared his throat. "Yes, we ... Amy and I want to announce our engagement."

No one said anything. They sat in stunned silence.

Mr. Spencer was the first to recover. "Well ... this is a surprise but let me offer my congratulations!"

"Yes, a surprise, although maybe it shouldn't be. I mean it could be hard ..."

"You mean because I'm a mulatto, Mrs. Spencer?"

"Yes, I'm sorry to say, but that's what I mean, the racial difference, that is …"

"We've thought about that, and we're prepared to face it," said Amy. She put her arm around her mother's shoulders.

"Where and when will the wedding be?" asked Mr. Spencer.

"Well, we're thinking spring, like Ed and Dorothea," said Amy. "But we can't get married in Ohio because the state has an anti-miscegenation law."

"What does that mean?" asked Marty.

"It means that the state doesn't allow marriage between people who are of a different race. Some other states have that law, too, but New York doesn't. We hope to be married there." Aron said.

"We might settle in Auburn where Harriet Tubman lives," Amy said. "Aron says people there are more accepting of differences."

"But if that shouldn't work out, we will migrate to Canada," said Aron. "But, of course, we'll be back to visit, or you can come visit us, if that happens," he quickly added.

"Well, it sounds as though you've given it a lot of thought. I wish you the best. When I think about it, it seems right. You two enjoy each other's company," Mr. Spencer said.

Virginia Spencer said, "Yes, Luke, I agree. I didn't mean that I was against the union. It's just that ... well, you know how some people are about race. For goodness sakes, we just fought a bloody war ..."

"We know, Mama, we know. I understand why you're concerned."

"This family will stand by you and help you any way we can. Aron is already like family." Mr. Spencer added his final blessing.

Amy and Aron looked at each other in what could have been interpreted as relief.

Amy said, "Oh, Daddy and Mama, I knew we could count on you."

The Writer and the Lover

Having admired John Rankin's anti-slavery letters, the autobiography of Frederick Douglass, and *Uncle Tom's Cabin* by Harriet Beecher Stowe, Marty had begun to try his own hand at writing. By lamplight in the evenings after helping build furniture, he was writing the story of what it was like to grow up in an abolitionist family. It was something he felt he was meant to do, just like Amy was meant to teach and Ed was meant to build things. He especially wanted to write about the trip to Atlanta to bring Ed home, but John Parker asked him not to publish such an account where it might be widely read, at least until more time had elapsed. He said there were still former slave hunters and slave owners who might hold grudges against him. It was disturbing to think about, but Marty did not want to do anything that could harm John Parker. Anyway, he just wanted to concentrate on the writing part for now. He would think about publishing later.

Marty also had something else occupying his thoughts. A slender girl with cornflower-blue eyes and sandy hair had his attention. She and her family were new to Ripley. Her brother had fought for the Union Army, and people said the war had left him "funny in the head." Marty had seen her in the store, patiently helping her brother do some shopping. She caught him staring at her and returned his look with a bold gaze that seemed like an invitation. He'd been daydreaming about how she would feel in his arms. Soon, he would get up his nerve to approach her.

PERSONAGES IN THE 1800's

John Brown (1800-1859); radical abolitionist who led an insurrection on a Federal armory, Harper's Ferry, VA

Levi Coffin (1798-1877); Quaker abolitionist in Indiana and Cincinnati, OH area

Stephen Douglas (1813-1861); American politician and lawyer from Illinois

Frederick Douglass (1818-1895); former enslaved man, abolitionist, orator, writer, and statesman

Frances Dana Gage (1808-1884); writer, feminist, and abolitionist

Ozem Gardner (1797-1880); abolitionist in Worthington and Columbus, OH

Benjamin Hanby (1833-1867); composer of "Darling Nellie Gray" and "Upon the Housetop"

Bishop William Hanby (1808-1867); a founder of Otterbein University; father of Benjamin Hanby, the composer

Abraham Lincoln (1809-1865); sixteenth President of the United States

Henry Wadsworth Longfellow (1807-1882); poet

John Hunt Morgan (1825-1864); a Confederate general, who led "Morgan's Raiders."

John Parker (1827-1900); abolitionist and former enslaved businessman in Ripley, OH

James Poindexter (1819-1907); minister, activist, Columbus, Ohio

John Rankin (1793-1886); minister, educator, abolitionist

Harriet Beecher Stowe (1811-1896); author of *Uncle Tom's Cabin*, pub. 1852

Charles Sumner (1811-1874); U.S. Senator from Massachusetts

Sojourner Truth (1797-1883); former enslaved woman, abolitionist, and feminist

Harriet Tubman (1822-March 10, 1913); former enslaved woman, abolitionist, and political activist

Nat Turner (1800-1831); enslaved man, preacher, leader of famous slave rebellion

John Greenleaf Whittier (1807-1892); poet and abolitionist

Clement L. Vallandigham (1820-1871); a United States Representative from Ohio and leader of the Peace Democrats ("Copperheads")

HISTORICAL EVENTS

1787

Northwest Ordinance regulated settlement in the Northwest Territory.

1793

First Fugitive Slave Act enacted.

1804

Ohio Black Laws enacted.

1820

Missouri Compromise declared free all territories west of Missouri and north of latitude 36 degrees 30'.

1847

Otterbein University founded.

1847-1857

Cincinnati Free Store sold only products made from slave-free labor.

1850

Second Fugitive Slave Act.

1854

Kansas-Nebraska Act; the fate of slavery left to local voters.

May 21, 1856

Lawrence, Kansas attacked by pro-slavery group.

May 22, 1856
Senator Charles Sumner, an abolitionist Republican from
Massachusetts, attacked by Representative Preston Brooks,
a pro-slavery Democrat from South Carolina, *with* a
walking cane.

May 24-25, 1856
Pottawatomie Massacre; murder of five men from a
proslavery settlement on Pottawatomie Creek, Franklin
County, Kansas., U.S., by an antislavery party led by the
abolitionist John Brown in retaliation for previous attack by
slavers.

March 6, 1857
Dred Scott decision, U. S. Supreme Court declared that
Scott, a slave who had resided in a free state, was not a
citizen and could not sue in a federal court.

Aug.-Oct. 1858
Series of debates between Stephen A. Douglas and
Abraham Lincoln.

October 16, 1859
Abolitionist John Brown led a raid on a Federal armory in
Harper's Ferry, VA.

December 20, 1860
South Carolina is the first state to secede from the Union.

April 12-14, 1861
Battle of Fort Sumter marks the beginning of the Civil
War.

January 1, 1863
President Abraham Lincoln issued the Emancipation
Proclamation. The proclamation declared "all persons held
as slaves within the rebellious states are, and henceforward
shall be free."

May 22, 1863
U. S. Government authorized the formation of the United
States Colored Troops (USCT).

September 2, 1864
General Sherman's troops capture Atlanta, GA.

November 15, 1864
General William Tecumseh Sherman started his march
from Atlanta, GA to Savannah, GA, ending December 21,
1864.

April 9, 1865
Gemeral Uysses S. Grant's army defeated Robert E. Lee's
army at Appomattox, VA. This battle effectively ended the
Civil War.

April 14, 1865
President Abraham Lincoln was assassinated.

December 6, 1865
The 13th Amendment to the U.S. Constitution abolished
slavery in the United States.

June 19, 1865.
Union General Gordon Granger gave an order declaring all slaves in Texas to be free, marking the legal end of slavery in the Confederacy. This is now celebrated as the national holiday Juneteenth.

PHOTOGRAPHS

Ozem Gardner House
8221 Flint Road
Columbus, OH
(2021)

Hanby House
160 W. Main Street
Westerville, OH 43081
(Westerville Historical Society)

John Parker House
330 N Front Street
Ripley, OH 45167
(September 2021)

John Rankin House
6152 Rankin Road
Ripley, OH 45167
(Courtesy of Ohio History Connection)

About the Author

Barbara Kussow is the author of a novel, *Portrait of Annie* and *The Merlin Subsidiary*, a collection of stories and poems. She is a contributor to *Writing after Retirement* (Rowman & Littlefield, 2014; ed. by Carol Smallwood and Christine and Christine Redman-Waldeyer). Her short fiction and poetry have appeared in online and print venues, such as *The Storyteller*, *Wild Violet*, *Mysterical-E*, *Kaleidoscope*, *Dos Passos Review*, *Hospital Drive*, and other literary magazines. Essays and book columns have appeared online and in local papers. Personal web site: https://bkussow.com

www.ingramcontent.com/pod-product-compliance
Lightning Source LLC
Chambersburg PA
CBHW070943180726
48291CB00004B/1112